U0461512

Peter Xu

林苑『双龙』译丛

总主编〇许景城

吉莲·克拉克

诗歌精选译介

基于人类世生态诗学视角

〔英〕吉莲·克拉克〇著

许景城〇译

汉英对照

The Selected Poems of Gillian Clarke

An Anthropocenic Ecopoetic Translation

(English–Chinese)

〇 Written by Gillian Clarke

Translated by Jingcheng (Peter) Xu

知识产权出版社

全国百佳图书出版单位

——北京——

This project is kindly sponsored by both the 2020 Programme
of Distinguished Young Talents in Higher Education of
Guangdong (Grant Number: 2020WQNCX014) and the 2023
Interdisciplinary Cooperation Programme of Guangdong
Planning Office of Philosophy and Social Science
(Grant Number: GD23XWW05).

本书获广东省普通高校青年创新人才类项目
（编号：2020WQNCX014）和广东省哲学社会科学规划
2023 年度学科共建项目（编号：GD23XWW05）资助。

For Professor Zhenzhao Nie and Ms. Xiaonian Tong

谨以此书献给恩师聂珍钊教授和师母童小念女士

Endorsements

This volume presents a selection of 80 English poems by the Anglo-Welsh poetess Gillian Clarke, thoughtfully translated and thematically arranged. Viewed through the lens of Ethical Literary Criticism, it reflects the translator's careful attention, deep passion and clear purpose, and effectively reveals the eco-ethical issues pertinent to Gillian Clarke's intricate relationships with nature, society, others and herself. It also conveys the poet's profound love for Welsh culture and customs, and her reflections on the ethical dilemmas and ethical choices brought to light by ecological crises in Britain and across the globe.

—Zhenzhao Nie, Foreign Member, British Academy;

Foreign Member, Academia Europaea;

Professor and Yunshan Chair of Foreign Literature and Language,

Guangdong University of Foreign Studies;

Emeritus Professor, Zhejiang University;

President, International Association for Ethical Literary Criticism

推荐语

　　这部诗集精选了英国威尔士女诗人吉莲·克拉克的80首英文诗，经过精心翻译并按主题编排成书，从文学伦理学批评视角看，此诗集体现了译者的用心、用情、用意，揭示了吉莲与自然、社会、他人及自我之间复杂的生态伦理问题，反映了诗人对威尔士风土人情的热爱，以及她对英国乃至全球生态危机所产生的伦理困境和伦理选择的关心和思考。

——聂珍钊，英国国家学术院外籍院士、
欧洲科学院外籍院士、
广东外语外贸大学外国语言文学学科建设
云山工作室首席专家和教授、
浙江大学荣休教授、
国际文学伦理学批评研究会会长

Peter Xu's ambitious project of translating Gillian Clarke's subtle and penetrating poems into Chinese is enhanced by an informative introduction on Welsh writing in English and on Clarke's poetics. Especially valuable is the emphasis on the ecocritical dimension of the poems. An impressive achievement.

—Derek Attridge,

Emeritus Professor of English at the University of York;

Distinguished British expert on literary theory;

Member, British Academy

Peter Xu's careful selection of eighty poems by Gillian Clarke, in his own ecopoetic interpretation, introduces her poetry to Sinophone readers, thus enriching their knowledge of contemporary British literature and helping build bridges between cultures.

—Galin Tihanov, George Steiner Professor of

Comparative Literature, Queen Mary University of London;

Member, Academia Europaea; Member, British Academy

This masterful translation captures the poetic essence and literary charm of Gillian's verses, offering readers a profound and evocative experience.

—Dongfeng Wang, Professor and Yunshan Chair

of Foreign Language and Literature,

Guangdong University of Foreign Studies;

Senior Translator entitled by the Translators Association

of China (TAC)

译者将吉莲·克拉克细腻深邃的诗作译成汉语，足见其满腔热血和豪情壮志，并在译者前言中翔实地介绍了英语书写威尔士这一流派和克拉克的诗学，实乃锦上添花，另外，凸显克拉克诗歌的生态批评维度，尤为可贵。此举着实出色、印象至深。

——德里克·阿特里奇，

英国约克大学英语荣誉教授、

英国当代著名的文学理论家与批评家、

英国国家学术院院士

译者精选了吉莲·克拉克的八十首诗歌作品，凭借生态诗学视角，向中国读者译介了吉莲的诗作，以期丰富读者的英国当代文学知识，助力搭建中英文化交流的桥梁。

——加林·提哈诺夫，伦敦大学玛丽女王学院

比较文学系乔治·斯坦纳讲席教授、

欧洲科学院院士、英国国家学术院院士

此书译笔娴熟精湛，捕捉到吉莲诗歌的诗韵精髓和文学魅力，为读者开启了一场意蕴深刻而思绪如潮的文学之旅。

——王东风，广东外语外贸大学

外国语言文学学科建设云山工作室首席专家和教授、

中国翻译协会（TAC）"资深翻译家"

Gillian is an iconic writer of pastoral poetry in Britain. Her poetic lines are brimming with the wildness and earthy scent of nature, addressing such natural beings as lands, valleys, rivers, marshes, islands, oaks, nettles, bonfires, stars, buzzards, foxes, starlings, and spiders, as well as such agricultural elements and activities as farms, fields, barns, farm equipment, and farmers. The poetess through her poems depicts a picture of the utmost sincerity, kindness, and beauty of the Welsh rural landscape, where her veneration for nature, respect for tradition, and yearning and pursuit for simplicity are manifest.

—Qingsong Li, Eco-literature writer;

Vice President of the Chinese Reportage Association;

Judge of the Sixth and Eighth Lu Xun Literature Prize

Dr Jingcheng Xu is devoted to the promotion of cultural exchanges between the East and the West by virtue of Chinese translation of English poetry. Achieving his PhD degree in English literature in the UK allows him to establish a solid foundation in English poetry. His accurate, vivid, and fluent translations become an ideal channel for Chinese readers to enjoy English poetry and understand the cultural ecology of English-speaking societies.

—Zhimin Li, Poet, Distinguished Professor of

Guangzhou Scholar in English Literature of Guangzhou University;

President of Guangdong Society of Foreign Literature;

Secretary General of China Association for Poetry Studies,

China Association for Comparative Studies of English and Chinese (CACSEC)

吉莲是英国具有代表性的乡村诗人。在她的诗中，充盈着自然的野性和泥土的气息。诗句涉及大地、山谷、河流、沼泽、海岛、橡树、荨麻、篝火、繁星、秃鹰、狐狸、椋鸟、蜘蛛等自然事物，也涉及农场、田园、谷仓、农具及农人等农业事物。吉莲的诗，构建了一种至诚至善至美的威尔士乡村图景。在这幅图景里，我们看到了她对自然的敬畏，对传统的尊重，对极简主义的向往和追求。

——李青松，生态文学作家、
中国报告文学学会副会长、
第六届和第八届鲁迅文学奖评委

许景城博士有志于通过英诗中译的途径促进中西文化交流。他在英国获得英语文学博士学位，具有扎实的英语诗歌功底。他的译文准确生动，可读性强，是中国读者欣赏英语诗歌并了解英语社会文化生态的理想渠道。

——黎志敏，诗人、
广州大学"广州学者"英语文学特聘教授、
广东省外国文学学会会长、
中国英汉语比较研究会（CACSEC）
诗歌研究专业委员会秘书长

Dr Jingcheng Xu's new book boasts a thoughtful selection and translation of Gillian Clarke's 80 poems and an insightful introduction that approaches the intricate relationships between nature, society, and individuals in the poetess's works through an ecocritical prism. It is a must-read, I believe without doubt, for anyone interested in poetry, translation, and ecological themes.

—Jie Zheng, Professor of Faculty of English Language and
Culture, Guangdong University of Foreign Studies

Dr Jingcheng Xu pursued his doctorate degree in Wales, researching modern and contemporary poetry from a Daoist perspective and addressing ecological issues in poetry. In this collection of Gillian Clarke's poems, the Welsh customs and ecological concerns, with which Dr Xu is familiar, echo mutually, and meanwhile the thematic arrangement of the collected English works with parallel Chinese translations enables readers to hearken to man and nature beating in the two languages.

—Xiaofan Xu, Associate Professor, School of English and
International Studies, Beijing Foreign Studies University;
Winner of the Eighth Lu Xun Literature Prize in Literary Translation

此书为许景城博士的最新译著，精心选译了吉莲·克拉克的 80 首诗歌，并附有一篇深刻的导言，从生态批评视角探究了这位女诗人作品中自然、社会与个体之间的复杂关系。这对诗歌与翻译爱好者以及对生态主题感兴趣的读者来说想必是一本必读的作品。

——郑杰，广东外语外贸大学
英语语言文化学院教授

许景城博士曾留学威尔士，研究现代诗与道家思想的呼应，并始终关注诗歌中的生态议题。在这部吉莲·克拉克的译诗选集中，许景城博士所熟悉的威尔士风土与生态关怀相互辉映，按主题划分、中英对照的安排又让读者得以听见人与自然在两种语言中的撞击声。

——许小凡，北京外国语大学英语学院副教授、
第八届鲁迅文学奖文学翻译奖获得者

Poetry plays an increasingly pivotal role in addressing ongoing environmental issues. Dr Jingcheng (Peter) Xu's book has introduced to Chinese readers the Welsh poet Gillian Clarke who exhibits in her works a strong passion for nature and nation. More importantly, he innovatively instils the idea of the Anthropocene in his translation practice. The translator's consummate skills and daring ambition, as I believe, will not only bring new lights into literary translations, but also provide significant inspirations for environmental protection. This poetic and timely publication truly merits perusal!

—Chao Xie, Associate Professor from the School of Chinese
Language and Literature, Central China Normal University

诗歌在应对当下环境危机中扮演着愈发重要的角色。许景城博士的译著为中国读者介绍了一位通过诗歌作品抒发对自然和民族强烈情感的威尔士诗人吉莲·克拉克。更为重要的是，译者在译介过程中创造性地融入了"人类世"这一概念。我相信，其高超的技巧和过人的胆识不仅会为文学翻译注入新的活力，同时也会为环境保护提供一些重要的启发。这本充满诗意且契合当下的作品值得细读！

——谢超，华中师范大学文学院副教授

Synopsis

An array of 80 well-chosen poems, written by Gillian Clarke, a prestigious Anglo-Welsh poet in the UK, from the late 1970s until the present, is displayed in this book. Taken from a wide spectrum of her anthologies, including *Snow on the Mountain* (1971), *The Sundial* (1978), *Letter from a Far Country* (1982), *Selected Poems* (1985), *Letting in the Rumour* (1989), *The King of Britain's Daughter* (1993), *Collected Poems* (1997), *Five Fields* (1998), *Nine Green Gardens* (2000), *Making the Beds for the Dead* (2004), *A Recipe for Water* (2009), *Ice* (2012), and *Zoology* (2017), these poems rich in theme are classified by celestiality and climate change, water resources, flora and landscape, animals, mineral ecology, geographical space and architecture, idyllic pastoralism, kinship and community, love and friendship, Welsh language, customs and festivals, music and sports, homage to historical figures, feminism, war and death, and international scopes. Whereas certain themes may be overlapped across a limited number of poems, a sense of growing depth and further exploration is collectively evident. Gillian's poetic works are in general characterised by their mellifluousness, dynamic imagery, emotional delicacy, linguistic freshness and simplicity, rhetorical uniqueness, and firm rootedness in reality without evading philosophical profundity and rumination.

内容简介

本译著精选并译介了英国著名盎格鲁－威尔士诗人吉莲·克拉克的 80 首诗歌作品，时间跨度从二十世纪七十年代末至今，选自《雪山》（1971）、《日晷》（1978）、《远乡来信》（1982）、《诗选》（1985）、《迎进流言蜚语》（1989）、《英国君王的女儿》（1993）、《诗选》（1997）、《五片原野》（1998）、《九座绿园》（2000）、《为死者铺床》（2004）、《水之秘方》（2009）、《冰》（2012）、《动物学》（2017）等诗集。主题丰富，涵盖天景与气候变化、水资源、植物与景观、动物、矿物生态、地理空间与建筑、田园牧歌、亲情与族群、爱情与友情、威尔士语、风俗节日、音乐与体育、怀古咏人、女性主义、战争与死亡、国际视野等。有些主题在部分诗中虽有所重合，却在某种程度上有所深化。总体而言，吉莲诗作富有音乐感、画面感，情感细腻，语言清新质朴，修辞新颖独特，内容贴近生活，却不失哲理，思想深邃。

An Introduction by the Translator

Gillian Clarke as a National Poet Writing for the Tribe and Welsh Ecology[①]

Jingcheng (Peter) Xu

If Dylan Thomas and R. S. Thomas stand out among the most prestigious Anglo-Welsh poets in twentieth-century Welsh literature, then Gillian Clarke has come to the fore as a vital and influential icon in the twenty-first century. Before exploring her poetry and poetics, it is of paramount significance to conduct a brief introduction to Welsh literature. This introduction will enable readers to contextually understand contemporary Welsh literature, especially Anglo-Welsh literature, in Britain. This contextualised understanding will furthermore facilitate a perception of Gillian's position in Welsh literature and her acceptance.

I Anglo-Welsh Literature

Welsh literature, as a type of ethnic minority literature, has in

---

① Originally published in Chinese from page 38 to page 50 in the sixth issue of *Foreign Literature and Art* in December 2016, this article is slightly revised and updated for this book.

译者前言

吉莲·克拉克：为族群发声、为生态言说的威尔士民族诗人 [①]

许景城 作

若说二十世纪威尔士文学史上最著名的盎格鲁 – 威尔士诗人代表是狄兰·托马斯和 R.S. 托马斯，那么二十一世纪最具代表性、最有影响力的盎格鲁 – 威尔士诗人之一便是吉莲·克拉克。详细介绍其作品和诗风之前，有必要先对威尔士文学做个简介，以便读者能大概了解当代威尔士文学，尤其是盎格鲁 – 威尔士文学在英国的地位，进而能理解吉莲在威尔士文学所处的地位与接受度。

一、盎格鲁 – 威尔士文学

威尔士文学作为少数民族的文学，向来被主流文学

---

① 此中文版本曾发表于《外国文艺》2016 年 12 月第 6 期，第 38 至 50 页，此处稍做修改和更新。

history been belittled within conventional and established literary paradigms. This belittlement continues in China as a result of restricted scholarly professionalism and translational capability in Welsh, as well as a prevailing favour for English literature in Britain. Even where Welsh poets are recognised in Chinese contexts, they are usually naturalised into the category of English literature rather than Welsh literature. As distinguished from this, Welsh-language literature within Wales has been flourishing, although a unique trajectory of development has characterised Welsh literature in English that emerged in the early twentieth century. The coinage of "Anglo-Welsh literature" by Harold Idris Bell (1879–1967) in 1922 described this literary movement. Debates have been triggered by the notion over time. As stated by David Lloyd, the term has been widely rejected because of its discerned post-colonial connotations, indicating Wales's thralldom to England, and therefore the alternative designation "Welsh Writer in English" has been chosen as a substitute of "Anglo-Welsh Writer".[1] Additionally, the term "Anglo-Welsh Writing" in comparison with "Welsh Writing in English" is likely to provoke slight uncomfortability among Welsh inhabitants, as it indicates that Anglo-Welsh writers do not either speak Welsh or regard themselves thoroughly English.[2] Therefore, such substitutes as "Welsh Writer in English", "Welsh Writing in English", and "Writing Wales in English" have received increasing

---

[1] LLOYD D. Welsh writing in English[J]. World literature today, 1992, 66(3): 436.

[2] KNIGHT S. A hundred years of fiction: writing Wales in English[M]. Cardiff: University of Wales Press, 2004: xi.

边缘化。国内一直以来对威尔士文学甚少关注与引介，这一方面源于能读、能译威尔士语的学者、译者甚少，另一方面在某种程度上也由于威尔士文学相对于英国主流的英格兰文学比较容易被忽略和边缘化，因此，即使国内学者关注，也是将所引介的威尔士诗人归于英国文学名下，而非威尔士文学。那么在英国又是何种情况？威尔士语文学在威尔士本土一直以来都在蓬勃发展，而发端于二十世纪早期的用英语写就的威尔士文学却面临着不同的命运。哈罗德·伊德里斯·贝尔（1879—1967）在1922年创造的"盎格鲁 – 威尔士文学"一词指代这一派文学。从诞生之初至今，此名一直备受争议。据大卫·劳埃德考究，诸多学者对该词持否定的态度，因其带有后殖民主义色彩，暗示了威尔士屈服于英格兰，故一些学者更多时候采用 Welsh Writer in English 来替代 Anglo-Welsh writer。① 另外，相对于 Welsh Writing in English 来说，Anglo-Welsh Writing 会让部分威尔士人感到不适，因为他们既不说威尔士语又不完全认为自己是英格兰的。② 因此，Welsh Writer in English、Welsh Writing in English 和 Writing Wales in English 是目前广泛被接受的术语。

① LLOYD D. Welsh writing in English[J]. World literature today, 1992, 66(3): 436.

② KNIGHT S. A hundred years of fiction: writing Wales in English[M]. Cardiff: University of Wales Press, 2004: xi.

acknowledgement.

It is at this juncture of imperativeness to review the definition of this type of literature. Glyn Jones denotes it as a piece of literary work by individuals written in the English language about Wales.[1] Michael J. Collins details Anglo-Welsh poetry as a kind of poetry in English by poets closely associated with Welsh past or those who regard themselves as an integral part of contemporary Welsh literature.[2] From these, it follows that this kind of literature refers to literary works by authors from within or beyond Wales, regardless of their competence and proficiency in Welsh, who navigate the past, present, and future of Wales by means of the English language. In light of this, Gillian is undoubtedly a representative of this trend. Born in Cardiff in 1937, she was so linguistically restricted to speak Welsh by her mother who distained the tongue that she failed to acquire Welsh as her first language but spoke fluent English. Yet, the defiance within the poet was ignited by her parent's "dominating" posture, driving her to learn her mother tongue.[3] As a Welsh-speaking poetess, Gillian has since then been voicing for her Welsh ethnic group via English as a medium of exchange.

Many insights have been offered in British academia pertinent to Anglo-Welsh literature, exploring its origin and evolution. A quite

---

[1] BROWN T. The dragon has two tongues: essays on Anglo-Welsh writers and writing by Glyn Jones[M]. Cardiff: University of Wales Press, 2001: 37.

[2] COLLINS M. Recovering a tradition: Anglo-Welsh poetry 1480–1980[J]. World literature today, 1989, 63(1): 56.

[3] WYLEY E. Review: very nice-not too Welsh[J]. The poetry Ireland review, 1999(62): 51.

在此有必要对该流派文学的定义做一番介绍。格林·琼斯将之定义为"威尔士个体作家用英语书写威尔士的作品"①。迈克尔·柯林斯进一步细化，做了如下定义，"'盎格鲁－威尔士诗歌'指的是与威尔士的过去有着千丝万缕、难以消融的关系或将自己看成目前威尔士文坛一部分的诗人用英语写就的诗歌"②。综合这些定义，我们可知，这一流派的文学是指出生在威尔士本土或之外的作家，不管本身是否以威尔士语为母语，用英语书写的威尔士过去、现在和将来的作品。吉莲的作品无疑就属于该流派。诗人1937年出生在卡迪夫，但从小被认为威尔士语难登大雅之堂的母亲禁止说威尔士语，所以诗人童年时并未习得自己的母语，而是说着一口流利的英语，然而母亲的"霸道"激发了诗人内心的叛逆，促使其去学习威尔士语。③此后，吉莲作为一名会说威尔士语的女诗人以英语为沟通桥梁不断为族群发声。

诸多英国学者对盎格鲁－威尔士文学提出了宝贵的见解，探讨了其起源和发展。对于该文学在二十世纪中

① BROWN T. The dragon has two tongues: essays on Anglo-Welsh writers and writing by Glyn Jones[M]. Cardiff: University of Wales Press, 2001: 37.

② COLLINS M. Recovering a tradition: Anglo-Welsh poetry 1480–1980[J]. World literature today, 1989, 63(1): 56.

③ WYLEY E. Review: very nice-not too Welsh[J]. The poetry Ireland review, 1999(62): 51.

comprehensive literature review is conducted in an article by David Lloyd on the advancement of Anglo-Welsh literature in the mid- and late-twentieth century. Concerning the origin of the genre, some scholars point at early twentieth century while others trace it far back to late fifteenth century. Quite informative overviews on this subject have been provided by Raymond Garlick and Roland Mathias in their respective books *An Introduction to Anglo-Welsh Literature*[1] and *Anglo-Welsh Literature: An Illustrated History*[2], as well as Michael J. Collins's work "Recovering a Tradition: Anglo-Welsh Poetry 1480−1980"[3]. Since this topic has also been reviewed in other relevant works, reiteration is avoided here. Nonetheless, what they have opined considering the introduction and recognition of Anglo-Welsh literature remains relevantly significant: some progress in the 1960s and 1980s notwithstanding, this type of literature has not gained adequate acknowledgement in Wales and beyond for multiple complicate reasons.[4] Although the global fame of poets like Dylan Thomas and R. S. Thomas has increased the popularity of Anglo-Welsh literature, the scale of its readership beyond Wales remains finite. A detailed exploration of the literature is offered in Glyn Jones's work *The Dragon Has Two Tongues: Essays*

[1] GARLICK R. An introduction to Anglo-Welsh literature[M]. Cardiff: University of Wales Press, 1970.

[2] MATHIAS R. Anglo-Welsh literature: an illustrated history[M]. Brigend: Poetry Wales Press, 1987.

[3] COLLINS M. Recovering a tradition: Anglo-Welsh poetry 1480−1980[J]. World literature today, 1989, 63(1): 56.

[4] LLOYD D. Welsh writing in English[J]. World literature today, 1992, 66(3): 437.

期和晚期的发展，大卫·劳埃德在其文章中做了详细的文献综述。对于该流派的起源问题，有人认为是二十世纪初，也有人认为是更早的十五世纪晚期。除此前提及的迈克尔·柯林斯的文章《回归传统：盎格鲁－威尔士诗歌 1480—1980》① 以外，雷蒙德·伽力克和罗兰·马蒂亚斯亦分别在其著作《盎格鲁－威尔士文学简介》② 和《盎格鲁－威尔士文学：详史》③ 中做了翔实的综述，此外还有其他一些著作做了相关介绍，在此不一一赘述。他们对盎格鲁－威尔士文学的译介状态所持的相同论断仍可沿用至今：尽管在二十世纪六十至八十年代取得一定的进展，却因诸多复杂因素未在威尔士本土和国际上获得足够认可。④ 随着狄兰·托马斯和 R. S. 托马斯在国际上逐渐享有知名度，盎格鲁－威尔士文学也逐渐被威尔士之外的读者所了解，但这种传播在广度和深度上还远远不够。格林·琼斯在二十世纪六十年代末编了一本比较详细的盎格鲁－威尔士文学集子，名为《龙有双舌：盎格鲁－威尔士作家和作品论文集》，里面除了涉及该文学流派的起源和发展，还着重向外界介

① COLLINS M. Recovering a tradition: Anglo-Welsh poetry 1480-1980[J]. World literature today, 1989, 63(1): 56.

② GARLICK R. An introduction to Anglo-Welsh literature[M]. Cardiff: University of Wales Press, 1970.

③ MATHIAS R. Anglo-Welsh literature: an illustrated history[M]. Brigend: Poetry Wales Press, 1987.

④ LLOYD D. Welsh writing in English [J]. World literature today, 1992, 66(3): 437.

on Anglo-Welsh Writers and Writing written in the late 1960s, introducing key writers from the early twentieth century to 1968 who primarily portrayed Wales in English, such as Caradoc Evans, Jack Jones, Gwyn Thomas, Idris Davies, as well as Dylan Thomas.[1] Of important note is that this kind of dissemination remains limited, with readership mainly confined to Wales.

There is only one monograph for the time being that comprehensively introduces Welsh literature in mainstream English-speaking academia beyond Wales, titled *The Cambridge History of Welsh Literature*, with around 860 pages, co-edited by Geraint Evans and Helen Fulton, and published in Cambridge University Press in 2019. Additionally, the "Writing Wales in English" project or centre to research and disseminate Welsh literature written in English has been established in key universities within Wales, such as Aberystwyth University, Bangor University, Cardiff University, and Swansea University (collectively known as ABCS). By virtue of what contemporary Welsh writers have resolutely contributed, such as Gwyn Thomas, Gwyneth Lewis, Gillian Clarke, Robert Minhinnick, and Angharad Price, Anglo-Welsh literature is reshaping the landscape of Welsh literature at an unprecedented rate, progressively cutting across local boundaries towards gobal visibility.

In 2013, a special issue titled "Contemporary Welsh Literature and Art" in *Foreign Literature and Art* was dedicated to introduce contemporary Welsh literature into Chinese contexts. "Thirty Years

---

① BROWN T. The dragon has two tongues: essays on Anglo-Welsh writers and writing by Glyn Jones[M]. Cardiff: University of Wales Press, 2001.

绍了从二十世纪早期到 1968 年期间主要用英语来书写威尔士的作家，包括卡拉多克·埃文斯、杰克·琼斯、格温·托马斯、伊德里斯·达维斯、迪兰·托马斯。[①]值得注意的是，这种传播还只限于威尔士本土之内。

目前，威尔士本土之外的英语主流学术界只有一套比较完整地介绍威尔士文学的英文专著，名为《剑桥威尔士文学史》，长达近 860 页，由杰兰特·埃文斯和海伦·福尔顿合编，于 2019 年由剑桥大学出版社出版。此外，威尔士本土几所主要大学 ABCS（Aberystwyth University、Bangor University、Cardiff University、Swansea University）相继成立了"英语书写威尔士"研究项目或研究中心，主要负责研究与传播用英语书写的威尔士文学。通过这些机构以及格温·托马斯、格温妮斯·路易斯、吉莲·克拉克、罗伯特·明黑尼克和安加拉德·普莱斯等著名的当代威尔士作家的不懈努力，盎格鲁－威尔士文学正以前所未有的速度重新书写威尔士文学，逐步走出本土，迈向国际。

2013 年，《外国文艺》出了专辑《威尔士当代文学与艺术》，专门向中国读者引介当代威尔士文学。其中一篇特约稿件《威尔士语当代文学三十载》比较系统地

---

① BROWN T. The dragon has two tongues: essays on Anglo-Welsh writers and writing by Glyn Jones[M]. Cardiff: University of Wales Press, 2001.

of Contemporary Welsh Literature" as a featured article in the issue systematically overviews contemporary Welsh literature, including Anglo-Welsh literature, and other articles unravell works by the contemporary Welsh poets and novelists as previously mentioned. Such a comprehensive introduction of contemporary Welsh literature to China is unprecedented, as stated by Hong Wu, editor-in-chief of the same journal. On May 2, 2014, a series of exchange activities to celebrate the special issue were co-arranged by Shanghai Translation Publishing House, Wales Literature Exchange, and the Confucius Institute at Bangor University.[①] During the symposium pertaining to Welsh Literature and Chinese Translation, participated scholars and writers attached importance to strengthen the promotion of Welsh literature in China. Hong Wu, the editor-in-chief, availed himself of this opportunity to call for greater attentions from publishing and academic circles in China towards Welsh literature. This was echoed by Sioned Puw Rowlands, former director of Wales Literature Exchange, who acknowledged the ensuing influence of the special issue and perceived it as a first step towards interpreting Welsh literature from Chinese readers' lenses. All these point to the great expectation and shared devotion of Chinese and Welsh-speaking British aficionados of literature to boosting the introduction and comprehension of Welsh literature in China.

---

① For more details, please see the news on the website of Bangor University. http://www.bangor.org.cn/news/2014-05-21/248.html. (Accessed on November 16, 2016)

介绍了当代威尔士文学和盎格鲁 – 威尔士文学的情况，其他篇幅还介绍了前面提及的当代威尔士诗人与小说家的作品。这种将当代威尔士文学较为全面地引介到中国的举动，套用《外国文艺》主编吴洪的话，"是史无前例的"。2014 年 5 月 2 日，上海译文出版社携手威尔士文学交流中心、班戈大学孔子学院共同举办了有关庆祝此专辑的系列交流活动。[①] 在当日下午共同探讨威尔士文学与中国翻译的圆桌会议上，与会学者一致认为有必要加强威尔士文学在中国的传播。吴洪主编以此为契机，呼吁国内出版界、学术界今后能更多地关注威尔士文学。威尔士文学交流中心前负责人秀内达·朴·罗兰斯对《外国文艺》的该专辑也表达了同样的期盼："借此专辑，我初步看到了如何从中国读者的视角来看我们的文学。"由此可见，中国和英国威尔士双方人士都急盼通过双方合作促使更多的威尔士文学引介至中国。

---

① 有关此活动的详情，请参看班戈大学的相关新闻稿。http://www.bangor.org.cn/news/2014-05-21/248.html。（网站访问时间为 2016 年 11 月 16 日）

II Literature Review on Gillian's Works

The special issue as aforementioned zoomed in on a single prose work by Gillian named "Voice of the Tribe".[1] Albeit bestowed with the title of the third National Poet of Wales after Gwyneth Lewis and Gwyn Thomas, Gillian has not garnered equal attention as regards translation, especially for her poems which are far richer and more remarkable than her prose-oriented works. Howbeit, attention and acknowledgement from British readers and critics have been growing for her writings, by virtue of her designation as the National Poet of Wales and the thematic diversity of her works. Her pivotal role is recognised as the founding director of Ty Newydd, an important writers' centre in North Wales established in 1990. Her influence on Welsh literature is accentuated by the incorporation of her poems in textbooks and exams for secondary education, as well as through invitations from the BBC to share her poetic works. Additionally, her accomplishments have been acknowledged with honours, such as the Queen's Gold Medal for Poetry in 2010. However, scholarship on her works within Britain remains narrow. An inclusive narrative of her achievements as a poet, editor, and teacher is accessible in the 1997 book *Trying the Line: A Volume of Tribute to Gillian Clarke*, compiled by Menna Elfyn, a famed contemporary Welsh poet. This compilation, aimed at celebrating Gillian's sixtieth birthday, comprises poetic works by R. S. Thomas, Seamus Heaney, and Carol

---

① CLARKE G. Voice of the tribe[J]. ZOU H, Translate. Foreign literature review, 2013(5): 25-31.

二、吉莲引介情况

《外国文艺》杂志《威尔士当代文学与艺术》专辑仅刊登了吉莲的散文随笔《族群之声》。[①] 作为继格温妮斯·路易斯、格温·托马斯之后第三位获得"威尔士民族诗人"殊荣的吉莲，在译介中遭到了不相称的对待，实属遗憾。吉莲的随笔散文集与她的诗集相比，在数量和知名度上都相差甚远。她的作品近年来获得了越来越多英国读者和评论界的重视与认可，一方面归因于其"威尔士民族诗人"的荣誉称号，另一方面归因于其作品主题的多样化。在北威尔士 1990 年成立的作家中心 Ty Newydd，吉莲被拥戴为第一任主席。其诗歌被纳入中学课本并列为考试内容，诗人经常受 BBC 之邀与读者分享她的诗歌和创作理念。2010 年，她获得英国女王"诗人金牌"奖章。目前，在英国学术界，对吉莲及其作品的研究相对来说还不算多。只有一本书籍较为系统地介绍了吉莲作为诗人、编辑、教师所取得的成就。该书由威尔士当代著名诗人蒙娜·尔芬于 1997 年在吉莲六十大寿之际汇编，名为《颂辞集》。这本集子收录的诗文多为吉莲的好友为她所作，包括 R. S. 托马斯、谢默斯·希尼、卡罗尔·安·达菲等所赠的诗，还有在诗人诗歌工作坊上过课的学生所写的回忆文章，以及一些针对诗人早期作品的评论文章。此外，一些著名的刊

---

① 克拉克. 族群之声 [J]. 邹欢，译. 外国文学评论，2013（5）：25-31.

Ann Duffy. Meanwhile, it harbours recollections from her students at her poetry workshops, and critiques on her earlier literary works. Besides, scholarly articles and book reviews have been published by reputable journals, exploring different aspects of her works, revolving around themes such as place, gender, Welsh identity, and nationality.

However, both Britain and China see a glaring gap in the scholarship of ecocriticism respecting Gillian's works. Her poetry continues the tradition of Welsh literature that pivots around pastoral and nature themes. However, there have been misconceptions of her portrayal of nature as a manner of escapism.[1] The similar misunderstanding of nature writing is clearly stated by the poet Neil Ashley, in his edited anthology *Earth Shattering: Ecopoems* that "Before the environment became a pressing issue of global importance, nature poetry was increasingly viewed as irrelevant", and that even if it was academically explored, negative reviews ensued, contrasting them with urban civilisation and regarding them escapist and old-fashioned.[2] Here Neil foregrounds the historical antecedency of nature poetry over environmental criticism but deplores the insufficiency of academic attention. Accordingly, he intentionally enriches his aforementioned collection of works from ancient to modern poets, spanning from East to West, encompassing Chinese poets such as Qian Tao and Bai Li, so as to re-ignite scholars' and readers' interest in nature poetry. Of interesting note

① HE N. The national depictions in the poetry of Gillian Clarke and Gwyneth Lewis[J]. Foreign literature review, 2013(1): 68.

② ASHLEY N. Earth shattering: ecopoems[M]. Northumberland: Bloodaxe Books, 2007: 15.

物还刊登过相关的学术文章和书评，研究大多数是从地方、性别、威尔士身份、民族性等角度出发的。

　　目前，不管在英国本土还是在中国，鲜有文献从生态批评视角去研究吉莲的作品。威尔士文学向来有注重牧歌、自然的传统，吉莲在其作品中也继承了这一传统。但是，她描写自然的作品被一些学者误以为是逃避现实的表现。[①] 这种对自然写作的类似误读正如《地球支离破碎》生态诗选集的编者、诗人尼尔·阿什利所言，"在环境成为亟须解决的全球性问题之前，自然诗歌日渐被认为毫不相关"，即使关注，也只是负面的评价，将它们与所谓的城市文明形成对照，认为作品逃避现实，陈旧老套。[②] 尼尔此处所强调的是，在环境批评进入评论视域之前，自然诗歌早已存在，只是未得到学者的有效关注。因此，为了方便更多学者和读者有效地关注自然诗歌，他在《地球支离破碎》中收录了诸多相关作品，覆盖的诗人从古到今，从西方到东方，包括中国的陶潜、李白等诗人。然而，他对威尔士文学的关注还是甚少，仅将 R. S. 托马斯的一首诗收入其册，就连

① 何宁. 论基莲·克拉克和格温妮丝·路易斯诗歌中的民族性书写 [J]. 外国文学评论，2013（1）：68.

② ASHLEY N. Earth shattering: ecopoems[M]. Northumberland: Bloodaxe Books, 2007: 15.

is that he draws little attention to Welsh literature, with a focus on a single poem by R. S. Thomas. Regardless of these efforts, works of influential Welsh writers like Dylan Thomas and Gillian Clarke remain ignored, conceivably as a result from spatial restraints, copyright issues, and an insensate post-colonial prejudice against Welsh literary accomplishments. My translation experience and archival research admit Gillian's advocacy for natural ecology and immaculate unification with her Welsh tribe within a large variety of her works which offer insights and admonishments for contemporary ecological crises.

Among early Chinese researchers of Welsh poetry is Professor Ning He, from Nanjing University's School of Foreign Studies. His scholarly achievements encompass three published papers in respect of this topic, where he initially introduces Gillian to Chinese readers from an ethnic perspective, while dedicating a limited portion of space to his general analysis of a comparatively limited range of her poetry. In his 2013 article, he opines that Gillian's poetic works, although deeply impacted by Welsh literary traditions, are confronted with shortcomings compared to those by other contemporary Welsh poets, especially considering her narrow vision, literary focus merely on rural Wales and pastoral traditions, insufficient cognition of the evolving nature and resistance forms of her nation and culture, and the evident lack of radical feminism in her disobedience of the patriarchal society.[①] Contradictory to his viewpoint, my opinion will

① HE N. The national depictions in the poetry of Gillian Clarke and Gwyneth Lewis[J]. Foreign literature review, 2013(1): 68.

名满国际的狄兰·托马斯的作品也未被收录，更不用说吉莲的作品了。这种无意识的编排，不仅是由于版面空间和版权的原因，更深层次上无疑是潜意识中典型的后殖民主义心态，不甚认可威尔士文学作品。其实通过翻译和研究，笔者发现诗人的作品大多为生态言说，与族群生死与共，用生命谱写并奏响生态乐章，其生态思想对当代生态危机有着积极的警示意义。

　　南京大学外国语学院何宁教授是国内较早关注威尔士诗歌的学者之一，至今共发表了三篇相关学术文章。他也是第一位学术性地从民族性角度将吉莲引介到国内的学者。不过何宁教授也只是用了较少的篇幅笼统地介绍和分析了诗人的一些作品。在其 2013 年的一篇文章中，他认为吉莲的诗歌深受威尔士文学传统的影响，但相对于其他几位当代威尔士诗人，吉莲的视野相对较小，本土化局限于威尔士的农村和对过去牧歌传统的依恋，缺少对民族和文化的不断演变和反抗形式的认识，反抗父权社会的女权思想不够激进。[①] 笔者对此持有不同观点，详见下文。

---

① 何宁.论基莲·克拉克和格温妮丝·路易斯诗歌中的民族性书写 [J].外国文学评论，2013（1）：68.

be detailed in the following section.

Ⅲ Gillian's Poetics

Since the 1960s, Gillian has been committed to poetic writing, publishing more than ten anthologies, encompassing *Snow on the Mountain* (1971), *The Sundial* (1978), *Letter from a Far Country* (1982), *Selected Poems* (1985), *Letting in the Rumour* (1989), *The King of Britain's Daughter* (1993), *Collected Poems* (1997), *Five Fields* (1998), *Nine Green Gardens* (2000), *Making the Beds for the Dead* (2004), *A Recipe for Water* (2009), *Ice* (2012), and *Zoology* (2017). These works as a whole mark Gillian's development from womanhood and motherhood to poeticality, a transformation defined by a changing focus from natural to urban ecology in Wales and from local to global visions. Although each displays features of its own, these collections collectively manifest themes centring on Wales, with nature as a main thread connecting urban and rural landscapes, and interior and exterior domains. The central themes are of richness, including celestiality and climate change, water resources, flora and landscape, animals, mineral ecology, geographical space and architecture, idyllic pastoralism, kinship and community, love and friendship, Welsh language, customs and festivals, music and sports, homage to historical figures, feminism, war and death, and international scopes, such as the Chernobyl nuclear incident and the advocacy for environmental protection. Whereas certain themes may be overlapped across a limited range of poems, a sense of growing depth

三、吉莲诗学理念

　　诗人从二十世纪六十年代开始投身诗歌写作事业，至今出版了十多部诗集，分别为《雪山》（1971）、《日暑》（1978）、《远乡来信》（1982）、《诗选》（1985）、《迎进流言蜚语》（1989）、《英国君王的女儿》（1993）、《诗选》（1997）、《五片原野》（1998）、《九座绿园》（2000）、《为死者铺床》（2004）、《水之秘方》（2009）、《冰》（2012）、《动物学》（2017）等。这些诗集整体上既反映了吉莲从女性、母亲到诗人角色的转变，同时也反映了诗人从关注威尔士自然生态到城市生态的转变，从本土视角到国际视角的转变。每部诗集都有各自的特点，总体上诗集所关注的主题以威尔士为核心，以自然为纽带，连接城乡及内外地域，呈现出多样化的主题，涵盖天景与气候变化、水资源、植物与景观、动物、矿物生态、地理空间与建筑、田园牧歌、亲情与族群、爱情与友情、威尔士语、风俗节日、音乐与体育、怀古咏人、女性主义、战争与死亡、国际视野（如切尔诺贝利核事件及呼吁环境保护）等。当然每部诗集中有些主题有所重合，但有深化，主题有机统一，形成"自然—人—语言"三位一体的主题框架，构建了一个为族群发声、为生态言说的思想价值体系。诗人作品富有音乐感、画面感，情感细腻，语言清新质

and further exploration is collectively evident. This organic unity facilitates the formation of a thematic trio of "nature – people – language", representing a broad-based system of thought and values reflecting the Welsh community and ecology. Gillian's poetic works are in general characterised by their mellifluousness, dynamic imagery, emotional delicacy, linguistic freshness and simplicity, rhetorical uniqueness, and firm rootedness in reality without evading philosophical profundity and rumination.

Gillian's poetry is greatly impacted by Wales's natural landscape, clearly mirroring her strong attachment to Wales's poetic tradition. Interviewed by *Sheer Poetry*, a popular British website on poetry, on August 24, 2005, she underlined the importance of poetry in Wales, arguing that "Poetry is the national art in Wales. It's an unbroken ancient tradition. I'm born into a Welsh tradition." [1] This ingrained national pride influences her poetic themes, particularly in her early anthologies such as *Snow on the Mountain* (1971), *The Sundial* (1978), and *Selected Poems* (1985), which mainly delve into the Welsh countryside and its customs, inspired by pastoral and elegiac traditions. Apart from her literary concern, Gillian also embraces an idyllic lifestyle. Albeit she was born in Cardiff and experienced urban life, the poetess longs for the serenity of rural Welsh living. Currently living in a smallholding in Ceredigion, central Wales, she observes amusingly that "I do live in the country. We have about eighteen acres and sheep—but this just leads everybody to believe—

---

[1] https://literature.britishcouncil.org/writer/gillian-clarke.(Accessed on September 7, 2016)

朴，修辞新颖独特，内容贴近生活，却不失哲理，思想深邃。

　　吉莲的诗歌比较侧重于对威尔士自然风景的书写，主要源自她对威尔士诗歌传统的重视。2005年8月24日，诗人接受了英国一个深受读者喜爱、名为《纯粹诗歌》的诗歌网站的采访。在采访中，她直言不讳："诗歌是威尔士的民族艺术。这种诗歌传统古老而延绵不绝，从无中断。我生于威尔士这个传统。"[①] 这种民族自豪感，始终影响着她的诗歌主题，尤其是她的早期作品，如《雪山》(1971)、《日晷》(1978)、《诗选》(1985)等。这些作品关注威尔士乡村风土人情，秉承牧歌、哀歌传统。在现实中，诗人也践行这种田园生活。诗人虽生于卡迪夫，并曾在大城市工作过，却向往威尔士乡村生活的恬适。她如今居住在威尔士中部锡尔迪金郡的一个小农场，过着牧歌般的生活。诗人曾用幽默的口吻描述自己的乡村生活："我住在乡村。我们大约有十八亩地和羊——但这就会让人认为——和声

————————————

① https://literature.britishcouncil.org/writer/gillian-clarke。（网站访问时间为2016年9月7日）

and state—that I am a rural poet. If you're a rural poet it means that you actually have to depend on the sheep for a living." [1] Apparently, Gillian accepts with pleasure to be labelled as a "rural poet".

The poem "Blaen Cwrt" recalls tranquil country life in Welsh valleys, registering a vivid description of local life contradictory to the fast-paced contemporary society. This contrast indicates a longing for a simple living, serving as a panacea for those entrenched by materialistic aspiration. The poem suggests that contentedness is sought in viewing the "Light on uncountable miles of mountain / From a big, unpredictable sky / Two rooms" that are completely adequate. The nub of human existence, as the poet maintains it, can boil down to the essential states of "waking or sleeping", entirely free from surplus desires. "To work hard", one can fulfil "the basic need" "in order to survive". In this sense, the poetess, who is aligned with R. S. Thomas as a fellow dweller of serene and peaceful rural Wales, is very likely to be viewed as a romantic lyricist committed to the depiction of Wales's natural ecology.

Dissimilar to R. S. Thomas, who rejected modernity in favour of solitude, Gillian has never isolated herself completely like a recluse. In her acknowledgement, "We have email, and we travel a lot" [2]. Frequent travels and correspondences with others through E-mail enable her to maintain and enhance her consciousness of Wales,

---

[1] WYLEY E. Review: very nice – not too Welsh[J]. The poetry Ireland review, 1999(62): 54-55.

[2] WYLEY E. Review: very nice – not too Welsh[J]. The poetry Ireland review, 1999(62): 55.

称——我是一名乡村诗人。如果你是乡村诗人，那就意味着你实际上不得不依赖这些羊来谋生。"[1] 可见，诗人实际上欣然接受"乡村诗人"的称号。

在《布蓝科特》这首诗中，她追忆威尔士山谷宁静的乡村生活，记录了远离现代化社会的翠烟袅袅的当地生活面貌。同时也表达了对极简主义生活的向往，给那些追逐奢侈生活的当代人一针强静剂：望着"山川绵延万里，光芒四射 / 天空浩瀚深邃 / 两个房间"足矣，因为人的生活本真无非"或醒""或睡"这两种基本状态，无需太多奢望，只要"努力劳作"，满足"基本需求"，"以便存活"。从这一角度看，诗人与一生居住在宁静威尔士乡村的 R. S. 托马斯一样，可谓是一位投身威尔士自然生态书写的浪漫抒情诗人。

然而与反对现代性和都市喧嚣以至于离群索居的 R. S. 托马斯不同，吉莲并非完全是与世隔绝的隐士。正如她坦言，自己"也用电子邮件，并经常旅行"[2]。由于经常旅行，并且与外界通信，她了解威尔士甚至世界的动态以及当代严峻的生态危机。因此，她的作品也开始

[1] WYLEY E. Review: very nice-not too Welsh[J]. The poetry Ireland review, 1999(62): 54-55.

[2] WYLEY E. Review: very nice-not too Welsh[J]. The poetry Ireland review, 1999(62): 55.

the world at large, and even serious ecological crises of the times. She started to devote her poetry to the increasingly urgent realistic ecological issues, with her anthology published in 1998, called *Five Fields*, marked as a turning point. Most of the poems in it evolve from pastoral themes to revolve around human existence in nature, exploring the issues of life and death, and notably expanding Gillian's portrayal framework of environmental places to include elements of urban ecology as well as rural, family, pasture, and farm environments that feature her early poetic works. Relevant examples include "The Field-Mouse", the first poem in the collection, which registers the conflict transpiring in Yugoslavia in the 1990s, and another poem named "A Difficult Birth, Easter 1998", concerning the city of Belfast, which relates a difficult cow birth to political issues in Ireland. Gillian's poetry has been since then concerned with not only rural Wales and familial issues but also urban ecological affairs and heatedly-debated international topics, transcending the geographical scope from regional Wales to international places. This is evidenced in the comment about Gillian made by Robert Minhinnick in 2004 in his work *Turning Tides: Contemporary Writing from Wales* that "the places and contextual environments portrayed by Gillian range from Wales to Bosnia and the Mediterranean coast, and the topics in recent years encompass war and terrorism" [1].

① MINHINNICK R. Turning tides: contemporary writing from Wales[M/OL]. Cardiff: Wales Arts International, 2004: 54[2016-09-13]. http://www.wai.org.uk/publications/1601.

关注棘手的现实生态问题。1998 年出版的《五片原野》是她诗歌主题的分水岭。该诗集中大多数作品从早期的牧歌模式发展演变到更多地去关注人类在自然中的生存境况，探讨生与死的主题，尤其地点环境描写的框架除早期作品以农村、家庭、牧场、农场环境为主之外，也加入了不少城市生态的元素。比如该诗集的第一首诗《田鼠》记录了诗人对二十世纪九十年代南斯拉夫暴力冲突事件对个人内心造成的影响。另一首题为《难产，1998 年复活节》的诗涉及贝尔法斯特城市，将母羊难产与爱尔兰的现实政治事件联系起来。此后至今，诗人的作品既关注威尔士的农村和家庭状况，也关注城市生态和国际热点。诗歌所涉及的范围不仅局限在威尔士，也涉及其他国际地域。这一点可以从另一位盎格鲁－威尔士诗人罗伯特·明黑尼克在 2004 年主编的《扭转潮流：威尔士当代作品选》中对诗人做的如下简介里得到印证："吉莲写了很多地方和背景环境，从威尔士到波斯尼亚和地中海沿岸，近来更是涉及战争和恐怖主义的题材。"①

---

① MINHINNICK R. Turning tides: contemporary writing from Wales[M/OL]. Cardiff: Wales Arts International, 2004: 54[2016-09-13]. http://www.wai.org.uk/publications/1601.

Gillian devotes various anthological works to speaking for ecology. The 1989 anthology *Letting in the Rumour* involves a poem named "Neighbours", which reflects not only the poetess's international scope, but also her concern with the global event of ecological crisis, i.e., the Chernobyl disaster. In the poem, Gillian's worry is clearly expressed pertinent to the global ecological deterioration generated by the nuclear-polluted air: the nuclear-contaminated air is prone to facilitate the transmission of the pollutants elsewhere, including Wales itself, because of bird migration and the global circulation of the air. This is evident in the poem's portrayal of the possible ramifications on local animals and residents within Wales: "Wing-beats failed over fjords, each lung a sip of gall", "a mouthful of bitter air from the Ukraine / brought by the wind out of its box of sorrows", and "a lamb sips caesium on a Welsh hill". Gillian concludes the poem with sympathy and condolences for the trauma and death brought about by the Ukraine nuclear catastrophe, admonishing that human beings should realise that "Now we are all neighbourly", living and dying together as part of the global community, and hoping that we as humans need embrace environmental protection urgently. This poem is realistically and meaningfully relevant to humanity on earth in the face of the potential nuclear calamity and hazard, and particularly in the context of the grand narrative of building a community with a shared future for mankind. Furthermore, in *Making the Beds for the Dead* (2004), there is a poem titled "On the Move" that depicts the ecological struggle of farm animals against aftosa or foot-and-mouth disease,

诗人在多部诗集中致力于为生态言说。1989年出版的诗集《迎进流言蜚语》中有一诗，题为"邻居"，该诗不仅反映了吉莲的国际视角，也体现了她对国际生态危机事件的关切，即切尔诺贝利灾难事件。诗人在诗中表达了对核爆造成空气污染而导致全球生态恶化的担忧：核污气体因候鸟迁徙和全球空气流通等自然现象定会将污染物扩散至其他地方，包括威尔士本土。这一点从诗中对威尔士当地的动物和人可能造成影响的描写可见一斑："振翼终结在峡湾上空，每个肺似呷一口胆汁""一口苦味浓郁的空气，源自乌克兰/由它那凄怆之盒放出的风吹来""一只羊羔在威尔士山岗上抿铙"。诗人在该诗的结尾对发生在乌克兰的核爆灾难给人们造成的创伤和死亡予以同情和悼念，警告人们须意识到"如今，我们互为睦邻"，作为人类命运共同体的一员彼此生死与共，并且她还希望人类应急切地拥抱环保理念。此诗对当今身处核危机和核威胁的地球人类来说，尤其结合构建人类命运共同体这一宏大叙事的背景来看，显得意义深刻。另外，2004年出版的诗集《为死者铺床》中有一首题为《迁移》的诗，就涉及农场家畜深受"口蹄疫"侵袭的生态困境，诗中处处彰显诗人对动物权利保护的生态伦理思考和人文关怀。此外，在2009年出版的《水之秘方》中有一组由八首小诗合成的题为《塞文河》的诗对源头在威尔士中部的塞文河的起源、神话传说以及流经地域生态问题进行了书写。2012年的作品《冰》

typifying her ethical concern for animal rights protection. In addition, her anthology, *A Recipe for Water*, published in 2009 comprises a set of eight verses titled "Severn", exploring the origins of the River Severn, its relevant myths and legends, and the ecological quandaries that confront the areas it passes. Her 2012 collection, *Ice*, is characterised by many hydrological depictions. All these poetic works exhibit Gillian's concern with real-life ecological issues, echoing what Professor Jonathan Bate, a prestigious British ecologist, in *The Song of the Earth* (2000), suggests: "What are poets for in our brave new millennium? Could it be to remind the next few generations that it is we who have the power to determine whether the earth will sing or be silent?"[1]. Evidently, Gillian as an eco-poet has been actively taking the ecological responsibility by addressing contemporary environmental issues and showing concern for the future of both natural and social ecologies through her poetry.

Meanwhile, the poet advocates for her Welsh tribe by means of integrating Welsh names of places and persons into her English poetry. This is partly due to her upbringing in a conflicting bilingual and bicultural environment. The dual confusion gives rise to her recognisation of the fundamental requirement for harmonising both languages, which is further evident in her autobiographical essay, named "Voice of the Tribe".[2] It is also partly as a result of Gillian's unique understanding of Welsh nationhood, as she clearly states

---

[1] BATE J. The song of the earth[M]. London: Picador, 2000: 282.

[2] CLARKE G. Voice of the tribe[J]. ZOU H, Translate. Foreign literature review, 2013(5): 28-29.

中亦有诸多关于水文生态的描写。这些作品对现实生态的书写，无形中响应了英国著名生态学者乔纳森·贝特教授在其 2000 年的著作《大地之歌》中的呼吁："在我们勇敢的新千禧之年，诗人能做什么贡献？是否能提醒今后的子孙，我们决定了大地将歌唱还是沉默？"[①]可见，吉莲凭借自己的诗歌力量承担起了当代诗人的生态保护之责，是一位不仅"出世"关注自然生态，同时又"入世"心系现实环境命运的生态诗人。

诗人同时也致力于为族群发声。她喜欢在英语诗歌中揉入威尔士的地名和人名。一方面，源于她从小生活在两种语言文化摩擦冲突的紧张关系中，因此感到困惑不已，并意识到应该为其找到一个平衡点，这点可以从她的自传散文随笔《族群之声》中得到印证。[②]另一方面，源于她对威尔士民族性的独特理解，正如她在《盎格鲁 – 威尔士评论》中所言："赞扬风景是远远不够的，因为威尔士不是由石头组成的，而是由人民和语言构成

① BATE J. The song of the earth[M]. London: Picador, 2000: 282.
② 克拉克 . 族群之声 [J]. 邹欢，译 . 外国文学评论，2013（5）：28–29.

in the journal *The Anglo-Welsh Review* that "It is not enough to praise landscape, for Wales is made not of stones but of people and language." [1] It is no doubt that she attaches great importance to Welsh identity and exerts efforts into the preservation of a distinct "Welshness" within her poetic works.

Preserving the Welsh language is a vital component of bolstering this "Welshness". The shrinkage of the Welsh language has been a pressing concern since King Llywelyn ap Gruffydd was defeated by King Edward I of England in 1282, resulting in a deprivation of political, cultural, and educational autonomy in Wales, thus leading to the shrinking prominence and purity of the Welsh language. Especially in the nineteenth and twentieth centuries, this issue intensified. By Tony Brown's account, from the 1870s, the *Education Act* was passed in Parliament, ensued by the *1889 Act*, which ordained English as the medium of instruction throughout Wales, expediting the corrosion of the Welsh language.[2] According to Michael J. Collins's statistics, in 1825, Welsh was spoken among about 80% of the Welsh population, but by the late nineteenth century, industrialisation and English immigration begot a decline, with only 40% Welsh speakers by 1915.[3] Based on David Lloyd's

[1] ELFYN M. Trying the line: a volume of tribute to Gillian Clarke[M]. Ceredigion: Gomer Press, 1997: 10.

[2] BROWN T. The dragon has two tongues: essays on Anglo-Welsh writers and writing by Glyn Jones[M]. Gardiff: University of Wales Press, 2001: xiii.

[3] COLLINS M. Keeping the flag flying: Anglo-Welsh poetry in the twentieth century[J]. World literature today, 1982, 56(1): 36.

的。"① 可见，吉莲重视威尔士身份，在诗歌中努力保持着独特的"威尔士性"。

对威尔士语的保护正是"威尔士性"的一个重要表现。自从 1282 年英格兰国王爱德华一世打败威尔士国王卢埃林，威尔士便失去了政治、文化、教育上的独立性，威尔士语开始逐渐失去原有的优越性和纯粹性。尤其当历史车轮滚进十九、二十世纪，威尔士语面临的危机愈加严重。据托尼·布朗记载，从十九世纪七十年代开始，威斯敏斯特议会通过《教育法案》，规定普及国立中学教育，之后《1889 年法案》规定威尔士普及国立中学教育而且必须用英语授课，不鼓励学生使用母语。② 根据迈克尔·柯林斯统计，1825 年，威尔士有大约 80% 的人口在说本族语言，然而到了十九世纪后期，随着威尔士迅速工业化以及大量的英格兰人入驻威尔士境内，说威尔士语的人数稳步下降，到了 1915 年，仅大约 40% 的威尔士人口说本族语。③ 据大卫·劳埃德 1992 年

① ELFYN M. Trying the line: a volume of tribute to Gillian Clarke[M]. Ceredigion: Gomer Press, 1997: 10.

② BROWN T. The dragon has two tongues: essays on Anglo-Welsh writers and writing by Glyn Jones[M]. Gardiff: University of Wales Press, 2001: xiii.

③ COLLINS M. Keeping the flag flying: Anglo-Welsh poetry in the twentieth century[J]. World literature today, 1982, 56(1): 36.

1992 data, there were approximately 500,000 Welsh speakers among Wales's 2.5 million residers.[1]

Those data indicate a downward trend and an increasing concern surrounding the status quo of Welsh speakers in the entire Welsh population. However, since the inception of Welsh nationalism and the Welsh language campaigning movement in the middle and late twentieth century, an expanding range of writers such as Glyn Jones, Ned Thomas, Jeremy Hooker, Tony Curtis, as well as Gillian, have collectively exerted great endeavours to preserve their mother tongue. Gillian, resembling R. S. Thomas, although commencing learning Welsh in her adulthood[2], underlines the significance of Welsh education for Wales's future, which dovetails with Gwyn Williams's statement that language is indispensably connected with national destiny[3]. In this regard, Gillian actively championed "Welshness" and the preservation of the Welsh language, as evidenced by her heartfelt speech at the opening ceremony of the meeting concerning "New Welsh Language Act" held in Cardiff in 1985.

This kind of advocacy is exhibited in her poetic works. In her anthology titled *A Recipe for Water*, there is a poem called "Welsh" that pithily substantialises the abstract concept of "Welshness" across various aspects of daily life. As the poem shows, the Welsh language within Wales is omnipresent, clearly demonstrated in the names of

---

[1] LLOYD D. Welsh writing in English[J]. World literature today, 1992, 66(3): 435.

[2] LLOYD D. Welsh writing in English[J]. World literature today, 1992, 66(3): 436.

[3] WILLIAMS G. The land remembers[M]. London: Faber & Faber, 1977: 16.

的统计，威尔士 250 万人口中只有大约 50 万人会说威尔士语。[①]

通过这些数据，我们可知，会说威尔士语的人口占威尔士总人口的比例逐年下降。状况着实令人担忧。但随着二十世纪中后期威尔士民族主义意识不断觉醒和"威尔士语言运动"的兴起，越来越多的威尔士文学作家，比如格林·琼斯、纳德·托马斯、吉瑞米·胡克和托尼·克蒂斯，开始担负起保护威尔士语的责任，吉莲也不例外。尽管她像 R. S. 托马斯一样成年后才开始学习威尔士语[②]，但她深信威尔士的光明未来在于坚守威尔士语的教育。这一点她也是继承了威尔士著名诗人、学者格温·威廉姆斯的观点："语言和民族命运密不可分。"[③] 因此，1985 年在卡迪夫召开的"新威尔士语言法案"大会的开幕式上，她慷慨激昂地呼吁坚守"威尔士性"和保护威尔士语的重要性。

她在诗歌中落实了自己的呼吁。《水之秘方》中的一首诗《威尔士语》，以小见大，将抽象的"威尔士语"一词具体化在生活的方方面面。威尔士语无处不在，大到郊区的名字，小到房屋的名字。威尔士语刻入自然生态中，与河流生息与共，同时也融入社会文化生活中，

① LLOYD D. Welsh writing in English[J]. World literature today, 1992, 66(3): 435.

② LLOYD D. Welsh writing in English[J]. World literature today, 1992, 66(3): 436.

③ WILLIAMS G. The land remembers[M]. London: Faber & Faber, 1977: 16.

suburbs and houses, and by its integration into the natural ecology, aligning itself with the fate of rivers, and also its incorporation into the social and cultural life. The significance of the language is manifest towards the end of the poem, which registers how it is rooted in local residents' DNA and also in their commonly-seen expressions of joy and celebration, such as the "shimmy and shout in Welsh in a Cardiff square". From this, it follows that the poetess interprets "Welshness" as not simply a linguistic identity but also a way of life, like the Welsh language innately knitted into the tapestry of daily existence. This association and identification by Gillian affirm the inextricability between the Welsh language and the wider notion of "Welshness".

However, Gwyn Jones might not endorse Gillian's identification of the Welsh language with "Welshness". In Jones's view, a Welsh poem composed in English, like Gillian's, fails to reveal the real essence of "Welshness" in that he opines that the Welsh language is an indispensible medium to maintain the authentic "Welshness" of Welsh literature.[①] By contrast, Gillian is very likely to distain this outmoded dogma, arguing that Welsh literature exploring Welsh customs and people through the medium of the English language, apart from the Welsh one, also harbours the capability of authentically capturing the essence of "Welshness", and that the English language is also effective to augment the significance and

① JONES G. The first forty years: some notes on Anglo-Welsh literature [G]// ADAMS S, HUGHES G R. Triskel one: essays on Welsh and Anglo-Welsh literature. Llandybie: Christopher Davies Publishers Ltd., 1971: 82-83.

正如诗歌末尾两句所反映的一样，威尔士语已融入人们的血液中，就连"在卡迪夫广场上／用威尔士语起舞呐喊，皆不以为奇"。由此可见，诗人将"威尔士性"不仅阐释为一种语言身份，而且也解读为一种生活方式，就像威尔士语常见于日常生活中。诗人将二者进行等同，认为二者息息相关，密不可分。

然而格温·琼认为二者并非等同。或许在格温看来，吉莲这样用英语书写威尔士语的诗并不能真正体现"威尔士性"，因为他认为具有"威尔士性"的威尔士文学必须是用威尔士语写就的。[①] 在吉莲看来，他的观点有些陈旧，真正具有"威尔士性"的威尔士文学并非一定要用威尔士语写就才能算是威尔士文学，也应包括用英语来书写威尔士风土人情的作品；此外，威尔士语的保护可以借助英语语言这一媒介，更好地向世界传递保护少数民族语言的重要性和急迫性。因此，从这一角度看，她更新和发展了格温·琼的观点。尽管诗人不能自

---

① JONES G. The first forty years: some notes on Anglo-Welsh literature [G]// ADAMS S, HUGHES G R. Triskel one: essays on Welsh and Anglo-Welsh literature. Llandybie: Christopher Davies Publishers Ltd., 1971: 82-83.

urgency of preserving minority languages, like the Welsh language. In this light, Gwyn Jong's belief is actually updated and developed by Gillian. Regardless of her incompetency to confidently compose works through the mere medium of the Welsh language, she displays her consistent pursuit for retrieving her own national identity by weaving and integrating Welsh elements into her poetry in English. In this sense, her endeavour to pursue a balance between varying perspectives from Gwyn Williams and Gwyn Jones is well evidenced. This synthesis of viewpoints embodies her unique understanding of Anglo-Welsh poetry.

Gillian's interpretation of "Welshness" is noticeable in her habitual utilisation of the first-person plural in such poems as "Blaen Cwrt" and "Community", substituting "I" for "we". This preference is entrenched, as she manifests, in the ubiquitous application of "we" in Welsh literature, dissimilar to the regularity of "I" in English literature, and it mirrors the collective sense of community deeply rooted in Welsh culture.[1] By harnessing the first-person plural, the poetess foregrounds the importance of familial heritage, the collective memory of past generations, and the identity of national tradition. Her goal is to awaken and rejuvenate the collective spirit of Wales as a national home, echoing China's constant emphasis on collectivism over individualism. Moreover, her effectual approach aims to distinguish Welsh literature from prevailing English literature, tacitly opposing its cultural and literary predominance.

[1] ELFYN M. Trying the line: a volume of tribute to Gillian Clarke[M]. Ceredigion: Gomer Press, 1997: 11.

1

信地用威尔士语从头到尾地进行写作，但她坚持在英语诗歌中穿插并融入威尔士语的写作方式也体现了她极力想找回自己的民族归属感。从这一层面上看，她在格温·威廉姆斯与格温·琼两位学者的观点中找到了一个平衡点。这反映了她对"盎格鲁－威尔士诗歌"有着自己独特的诠释。

诗人对"威尔士性"的诠释还体现在她的诗中经常使用第一人称的复数形式。在《布蓝科特》和《群居》两首诗中，她用"we"代替了"I"。究其原因，正如她自己所强调的，威尔士文学中用"we"非常普遍，不像英格兰文学那样用"I"的情况多，这主要源于威尔士更有"community"的集体主义感。[①] 通过第一人称的复数形式来叙事，诗人重在强调家族历史、几代人的集体记忆和民族传统的身份认同，希望唤醒和复苏威尔士民族的集体家园意识。这一点与中国历来强调集体主义而淡化个人主义是非常契合的。同时诗人的这种巧妙处理方式也意在将威尔士文学与主流的英格兰文学区别开来，算是一种对后者文化文学霸权的隐性挑战。

---

① ELFYN M. Trying the line: a volume of tribute to Gillian Clarke[M]. Ceredigion: Gomer Press, 1997: 11.

The poet's advocacy for the community is represented by her consistently moderate feminist view, and laudation of Welsh females. In Professor Ning He's view, Gillian's long poem "Letter from a Far Country" is a woeful lament of a rural domestic woman, typifying Gillian's feminist awareness.[①] Viewed through an ecofeminist prism, the 390-line poem builds an innate similarity between women and the Earth in destiny, decrying both the patriarchal domination of women and the human exploitation of the natural world. Meanwhile, examined from the perspective of material ecocriticism, the images mentioned, such as bottles and jars, in the female narrator's household, as well as a teapot in the wheat field, all point to sorrowful tales. All this substantiates Gillian's eco-philosophy, which positions females' existence within the wider natural environment. Just as Professor He argues, the poem from a female perspective pivots around the female narrator's mental state of displeasure and grievance against her daily mundane concerns.

Howbeit, a defect in his argument emerges from his disapproval with the moderate feminist viewpoint expressed in the poem. In his view, the feminist perceptions and behaviours conveyed are not radical or outright enough, and somewhat disappointing. Nonetheless, it is of great significance to recognise that Gillian purposefully weakens the female narrator's bitterness in the latter part of the poem and instead accentuates the vital contributions to the family made by her grandmothers and mother as females.

① HE N. The national depictions in the poetry of Gillian Clarke and Gwyneth Lewis[J]. Foreign literature review, 2013(1): 57-58.

诗人为族群发声还体现在她一向温和的女权主义观，以及对威尔士妇女的歌颂。何宁教授在解读《远方来信》时，认为此诗是农村妇女的闺怨诗，是诗人女权主义意识的表现。[①] 而从生态女性主义角度出发，不难发现诗人在这首三百九十行的诗中，呈现了妇人和大地之间的内在命运相似性，反对父权社会对女性的压制和人类对自然的剥削。从物质生态批评视角观看，亦会发觉此诗所描绘的女性叙述者家庭中的那些瓶瓶罐罐和麦田里的茶壶等物件背后无不隐藏并诉说着一段段辛酸的故事。这反映了诗人将女性的生存状况放在更大的自然环境背景中去考虑和诠释的生态理念。诚如何教授所言，诗人在诗中从女性视角出发细致入微地刻画了女性叙事者对生活琐碎之事产生的厌恶和抱怨的心理状态。

然而，何教授的不足之处在于，他不赞成诗人温和的女权主义观，认为此诗的女权思想不够激进，做法也不够彻底，对此他表示惋惜。但值得注意的是，诗人在此诗的后半部分弱化了女性叙述者的愤怒，追忆了祖母、母亲作为女性对家庭做出的伟大贡献。正如诗人自己在解释此诗创作背景时所说："该诗从开始的愤怒演

① 何宁.论基莲·克拉克和格温妮丝·路易斯诗歌中的民族性书写 [J].
外国文学评论，2013（1）：57-58.

The poet explains herself concerning the context of creating such a poem: "The poem that began in anger turned into a celebration." [1] This indicates the poet's intention of celebrating the endeavours of Welsh females in families. In addition, Gillian elucidates: "When I wrote this poem, in the late 1970s, it was my small contribution to the feminist debate. At the extremist end of 1970s feminism some of the argument was sad, simplistic and selfish, and as violent as the male world it attacked." [2] Apparently, Professor He fails to faithfully understand Gillian's feminist perceptions. It is commonly known that radical feminist conducts, through the prism of familial and social harmony, can generate further troubles and crises, intensifying familial and social discords, and prolonging social injustice. In this sense, Gillian's moderate view of feminism merits advocacy in pursuit of a harmonious world of our time.

Gillian's poetic style is featured by a natural, "down to earth" simplicity and purity. She harbours a unique prism into poetic language, regarding poetry as a gradual crystallisation of ideas admist the course of writing. In her explanation, "After pen and paper, the beauty of the empty cleanness, there is energy. It sets me thinking. I try the paper to see what the words will do. It must be like drawing ... try the line, see what happens" [3]. This approach is maintained in her

[1] http://www.sheerpoetry.co.uk/advanced/gillian-clarke/letter-from-a-far-country. (Accessed on January 3, 2016)

[2] http://www.sheerpoetry.co.uk/advanced/gillian-clarke/letter-from-a-far-country. (Accessed on January 3, 2016)

[3] CLARKE G. Interview with Gillian Clarke[G]// BUTLER S. Common ground: poets in a Welsh landscape. Bridgend: Poetry Wales Press, 1985: 198.

变成后来对女性所做的一切的赞扬。"① 这说明诗人是有意地去歌颂威尔士女性对家庭所付出的一切。诗人进一步解释："此诗是我于 20 世纪 70 年代末所写，算作我对女权主义辩论的一个小贡献。当时正值极端女权主义末期，有些争论令人悲痛、简单自私，且还像其所攻击的父权社会那般充满了暴力性。"② 显然，何宁教授并没有真正地把握诗人的女权思想。我们知道，从家庭、社会生态和谐角度出发，过激的女权行为会衍生出更多的问题与危机，激化家庭和社会矛盾，进一步导致社会不公。因此，诗人温和的女权观在当今和谐社会中是值得提倡的。

吉莲的诗风颇为"亲民"，朴实纯粹。她有着独特的诗歌语言观，认为诗歌从来不是将脑海中已有想法付诸笔墨而是思想在创作中逐渐形成："笔纸之后，空白干净之美中便有了能量。我试着写在纸上，想看看文字将如何发挥作用。它必须看起来像是在画画……画线条，看奇迹发生。"③ 她坚持这种创作理念，故其

① http://www.sheerpoetry.co.uk/advanced/gillian-clarke/letter-from-a-far-country。（网站访问时间为 2016 年 1 月 3 日）

② http://www.sheerpoetry.co.uk/advanced/gillian-clarke/letter-from-a-far-country。（网站访问时间为 2016 年 1 月 3 日）

③ CLARKE G. Interview with Gillian Clarke[G]//BUTLER S. Common ground: poets in a Welsh landscape. Bridgend: Poetry Wales Press, 1985: 198.

poetics, giving rise to poems devoid of conventional rhyme schemes but retaining vivid imagery. In M. Wynn Thomas's view, "Clarke is a painterly poet." [1]

Besides, Gillian views poetic language as both deeply rooted in daily life and imperatively refined to boost its poetic quality. Christine Ewans recalls Gillian's metaphorical words: "Having a good word in your head is like keeping a smooth stone in your pocket, to keep it warm and silky with stroking. Words like to be stroked." [2] This statement affectionately foregrounds the poet's belief in retaining the innate relationship of poetic language with daily life while also stressing the importance of perfecting language over daily expressions. Upon reading Gillian's poem named "Baby Sitting" for the first time, Christine was instantaneously arrested and amazed by its language. Incipiently, she doubted whether it could actually be called a poem; however, further scrutinisation allowed her to acknowledge Gillian's proficiency in articulating, by virtue of simple and yet accurate language, the real nuances in nursing sentiments from a mother to her own child and others'. [3] My own experience of translating this poem into Chinese and examining others by the same poet also informs that Gillian is such a poetess that unfailingly harnesses daily-life-rooted expressions and purposeful linguistic

[1] THOMAS M. Staying to mind things: Gillian Clarke's early poetry[G]// ELFYN M. Trying the line: a volume of tribute to Gillian Clarke. Ceredigion: Gomer Press, 1997: 53.

[2] EWANS C. Waking up the words[G]// ELFYN M. Trying the line: a volume of tribute to Gillian Clarke. Ceredigion: Gomer Press, 1997: 75.

[3] EWANS C. Waking up the words[G]// ELFYN M. Trying the line: a volume of tribute to Gillian Clarke. Ceredigion: Gomer Press, 1997: 76.

诗歌形式基本都是无韵散文体，却不失画面感。正如M.温·托马斯所言："诗人是一位画家似的诗人。"[1]

此外，她还认为诗歌的语言源自生活，但也须不断凝练，使其富有诗意。正如克莉丝汀·埃文斯回忆起吉莲隐喻化的观点："脑海中拥有好词就像口袋里装着一块光滑的石头，通过打磨让它不断发热，如丝般顺滑。语言就是需要打磨。"[2] 可见，诗人的诗歌语言观既强调诗歌语言与生活的紧密性，又强调语言高于生活、进行升华的必要性。因此，当克莉丝汀第一次接触诗人的诗歌《照看婴儿》时，被它的语言所震惊。她的第一感觉是怀疑这是否是诗，之后通过进一步细读，发现诗人的伟大之处在于通过平淡朴实却非常准确的言语说出了母亲照看自己的婴儿与别人的婴儿的不同的真实感受。[3]通过汉译此诗和对作者其他诗歌的研究，笔者发现这位女诗人确实始终在生活性的语言与凝练升华的语言之间做到了很好的平衡。

---

[1] THOMAS M. Staying to mind things: Gillian Clarke's early poetry[G]// ELFYN M. Trying the line: a volume of tribute to Gillian Clarke. Ceredigion: Gomer Press, 1997: 53.

[2] EWANS C. Waking up the words[G]// ELFYN M. Trying the line: a volume of tribute to Gillian Clarke. Ceredigion: Gomer Press, 1997: 75.

[3] EWANS C. Waking up the words[G]// ELFYN M. Trying the line: a volume of tribute to Gillian Clarke. Ceredigion: Gomer Press, 1997: 76.

refinement in perfect balance.

A proficient grasp of plain language that characterises Gillian's poetry is coupled with a keen and vital sense of life lessons. Her artistry revolves around integrating into her poems her personal experiences, and refining them to philosophical sagacity. Within her work named "Swimming with Seals" from the anthology *The King of Britain's Daughter* (1993), the poetess relates an experience of swimming with seals off Wales's west coast, masterfully interweaving two distinct worlds, above and underneath the water's surface. Her more profound understanding of the invisible aquatic "gardens of the sea" is dissimilar to that of the elderly individuals lying on the chair on the beach and seeing the sunset through binoculars, whose vision is limited to the blue realm where the heaven and the ocean meet. It is noted that towards the end of the poem Gillian stresses the ecological symbiosis between humanity and nonhuman animals: she, like the seals, experiences the ocean's maternal love, evocative of that of a womb's amniotic sac. In contrast to the recondite style of her precursor, Dylan Thomas, Gillian harnesses lucid language suffused with profound significance and realistic rootedness.

Her poetic style has obtained numerous high acclaims. As *The Listener*, a BBC magazine, speaks highly of it, "There is no gaudiness in her poetry; instead, the reader is aware of a generosity of spirit which allows the poems' subjects their own unbullied reality." [1] Likewise, the *Times Literary Supplement* celebrates her: "Gillian

---

[1] CLARKE G. Selected poems[M]. Manchester: Carcanet NewPress, 1985.

诗人平淡的语言中有着不同凡响的人生感悟。她擅于将所亲历之事件、人物融入诗中，最后加以升华，得出富有意义的人生哲学。比如，在 1993 年出版的诗集《英国君王的女儿》中有一首诗《与海豹共游》。此诗描述的是诗人在威尔士西部海域与海豹共游的亲历之事。她看到了海上和海下两个不同的视域，这与在沙滩躺椅上享受夕阳的老年人形成鲜明的对比，因为他们尽管举着望远镜却只能看到海天交接的蓝色地平面，而对于水下的"海中花园"般的蓝色世界，却视野受限，不像诗人有着真实的深刻体会。此诗最后几行还道出了人与动物的生态共源性：她与海豹一样，在犹如子宫的大海羊膜中享受着大海的母爱。可见，吉莲不像她的前辈狄兰·托马斯那样语言晦涩深奥，而是多了几分清澈隽永，趋于生活化。

吉莲的诗风得到诸多赞誉。BBC 旗下的杂志《听众》曾高度评价："她的诗歌基本没有诡异句法、俗艳辞藻，相反读者可以在诗歌中感受到一种慷慨的真情，这样诗歌主题就紧扣现实而不强迫现实。"[1]《泰晤士报文学副刊》也高度评论过诗人："吉莲·克拉克的诗歌

---

① CLARKE G. Selected poems[M]. Manchester: Carcanet NewPress, 1985.

Clarke's poems ring with lucidity and power." ① Different from Dylan's concentrated imagery and strict rhyme scheme, Gillian's poetry boasts a prose-like musical rhythm, as in the continuous description by the *Times Literary Supplement* of her "language as concrete as it is musical" ②. Regarding metrical and rhyming patterns, in addition to the unrhymed forms aforementioned, some of Gillian's poetic works inherit the tradition of Welsh poetry in terms of rhythm and rhyme. As Robert Minhinnick states, "She sometimes weaves characteristics typical of Welsh-language poetry, such as traditional strict metres, into her work" ③.

Conclusion

As a distinguished contemporary national poet of Wales, Gillian Clarke demonstrates a distinctive approach to the interpretation of Anglo-Welsh poetry, accentuating the representation of Wales by means of the English language and integration of Welsh elements. Simplicity, freshness, and linguistic potency are characteristic of her poetic works, which, register daily-life-rooted themes, arresting readers via vivid imagery and musical rhythms. As an adamant pioneer for Welsh identity, she puts her heart into the embracing of her nation's destiny, the contribution to its rejuvenation, the

---

① CLARKE G. Five fields[M]. Manchester: Carcanet New Press, 1998.

② CLARKE G. Five fields[M]. Manchester: Carcanet New Press, 1998.

③ MINHINNICK R. Turning tides: contemporary writing from Wales[M/OL]. Cardiff: Wales Arts International, 2004: 54 [2016-09-13]. http://www.wai.org.uk/publications/1601.

清澈回响，苍劲有力。"[1] 虽然不像狄兰的语言字字铿锵有力、意象浓缩、力求押韵，但她的诗给人一种散文般富有音乐节奏的体验，正如《泰晤士报文学副刊》所评论的，"语言形象具体，又富有音乐感"[2]。在格律方面，除以上提到的无韵体之外，诗人的一些诗歌作品在节奏和押韵方面也继承了威尔士诗歌传统，正如罗伯特·明黑尼克所言，吉莲有时"在她的英语诗歌中穿插着威尔士语诗歌独有的东西，比如传统的、严格的音步"[3]。

结　语

吉莲·克拉克是一位伟大的当代威尔士民族诗人。她用自己独特的方式诠释盎格鲁–威尔士诗歌，坚持用英语和威尔士语穿插的方式来书写威尔士。其语言淳朴清新、苍劲有力，主题紧扣生活，画面感强，富有音乐节奏感。她极力维护威尔士身份，心系民族命运和复兴，致力于保护威尔士语，歌颂威尔士女性，为族群发声。此外，她还是一位生态诗人，关注乡村自然风景、城市生态，带着既着眼本土又放眼国际的双重视野来歌

---

① CLARKE G. Five fields[M]. Manchester: Carcanet New Press, 1998.

② CLARKE G. Five fields[M]. Manchester: Carcanet New Press, 1998.

③ MINHINNICK R. Turning tides: contemporary writing from Wales[M/OL]. Cardiff: Wales Arts International, 2004: 54 [2016-09-13]. http://www.wai.org.uk/publications/1601.

preservation of the Welsh language, the singing of Welsh women, and the augmentation of her tribe's voice. Meanwhile, as an eco-poet, she revolves around rural landscape and urban ecology in her poems that offer both locally-based and globally-relevant viewpoints, echoing the beauty of nature and enhancing consciousness of environmental protection by ringing an alarm bell for ecological predicament. It is indubitable that Gillian's accomplishments shall be registered in the history of Anglo-Welsh literature, with her works noteworthy of the increasing attention and widening readership beyond Wales. China is thus hoped to witness enlarging readership and scholarship that appreciate and scrutinise the Welsh poetess's multilayered poetics.

Last but not least, the following figures merit my warmest acknowledgements. My initial gratitude goes to the poetess Ms. Gillian Clarke for her constant trust and support, and the publisher of her English anthologies for granting me the permission to translate her 80 poems into Chinese and publish the translations in parallel with the original English texts which constitute the present bilingual book. Many thanks are given to Ms. Hong Cai and Ms. Yi Yang from Intellectual Property Publishing House Co., Ltd., as well as Ms. Jingjing Chen, executive director and senior editor from Beijing Shiny Culture Co., Ltd., for their professional, meticulous, and responsible guidance, editing, proofreading, and feedback, which have facilitated the presentation of the book in exquisite manners. I am gratefully indebted to my dearest mentor Prof. Zhenzhao Nie, and other respected scholars, poets, friends, and peers, such as Prof. Derek Attridge, Prof. Galin Tihanov, Prof. Dongfeng Wang, Mr. Qingsong

唱自然生态之美，敲响了生态危机的警钟。诗人的成就定将在益格鲁－威尔士文学史上留下浓墨重彩的一笔。她的作品值得威尔士以外的读者认真学习和借鉴。此拙文乃抛砖引玉，希望国内能有更多的同行来关注这位女诗人并挖掘其更多的诗学理念。

最后，请允许我对如下人士表达最真诚的感谢。首先，感谢诗人吉莲·克拉克女士一如既往对我的信任和支持，感谢其作品出版方授权我对其八十首英文诗歌进行汉译，并同意以双语对照方式出版本译著。其次，感谢北京知识产权出版社蔡虹女士和杨易女士，以及北京浅汐文化有限责任公司执行董事、资深编辑陈晶晶女士，她们专业、认真和负责的业务指导、编辑、校对与反馈让本译著最终以最好的形式呈现。再次，感谢我最敬爱的恩师聂珍钊教授，以及其他备受敬重的学者、诗友、同人如德里克·阿特里奇教授、加林·提哈诺夫教授、王东风教授、李青松先生、黎志敏教授、郑杰教授、许小凡副教授、谢超副教授等为本译著撰写推荐语。另外，由衷地感谢一路给予过我启迪、帮助和鼓励的校级和院级的领导、同事和朋友。最后，感谢家人始

Li, Prof. Zhimin Li, Prof. Jie Zheng, Associate Prof. Xiaofan Xu, and Associate Prof. Chao Xie for their endorsements for this volume. Not less importantly, I would like to express my heartfelt thanks to the leaders, colleagues, and friends at both university and faculty levels, who have enlightened, helped, and encouraged me all the way. Ultimately, to my family, never are there sufficient words of indebtedness for their unswerving companionship, support, solace, and encouragement. It is with the assistance of all the aforementioned figures that this publication is possible. Be that as it may, errors and mistakes are unavoidable in this book as a result of the limitedness of my knowledge, capability, vision, and perspective. It is thus my earnest hope for inviting academic peers and readers in the field of translation studies and literature to offer criticism and suggestion if any.

终给予的坚定陪伴、支持、慰籍和鼓励。正是因为有了以上人士的鼎力相助，此译著才能最终顺利面世。然而因笔者学识、能力、视野和格局有限，本译著难免会有纰漏，恳请广大译界、文学界同人和读者不吝赐教。

Contents

Celestiality and Climate Change

Water Resources

Flora and Landscape

目　录

天景与气候变化

水资源

植物与景观

Animals

Mineral Ecology

Geographical Space and Architecture

Idyllic Pastoralism

Kinship and Community

Love and Friendship

Welsh Language

Customs and Festivals

Music and Sports

Homage to Historical Figures

威尔士语

风俗节日

音乐与体育

怀古咏人

Feminism

War and Death

International Scope

Bodnant Garden
For Gillian Clarke

博德南特花园

致敬吉莲·克拉克

Celestiality and Climate Change

天景与气候变化

The Sundial

Owain was ill today. In the night
He was delirious, shouting of lions
In the sleepless heat. Today, dry
And pale, he took a paper circle,
Laid it on the grass which held it
With curling fingers. In the still
Centre he pushed the broken bean
Stick, gathering twelve fragments
Of stone, placed them at measured
Distances. Then he crouched, slightly
Trembling with fever, calculating
The mathematics of sunshine.

He looked up, his eyes dark,
Intelligently adult as though
The wave of fever taught silence
And immobility for the first time.
Here, in his enforced rest, he found
Deliberation, and the slow finger
Of light, quieter than night lions,
More worthy of his concentration.
All day he told the time to me.

日晷

今日，欧文病了。午夜时分，
他语无伦次，在难眠的炎热中
嘶吼如狮。而今，他口干
舌燥，脸色苍白，用弯曲的
手指将一个纸环
放在草地上。在静止的纸环
中心，他推移残缺的豆
棒，集齐十二块碎石，
将其按一定距离排开
摆放。然后，发烧未退的他
俯身蹲下，微微颤抖地数着
日影，测算着时刻。

他仰望天空，双眸深邃，
带着成人般的睿智，仿佛
这波发烧的热浪让他初次
学会了沉默不语和纹丝不动。
此处，他被迫歇息，懂得
冥思苦想和光影指针
的慢移，相比一只只夜狮
则更加静谧，更值得专心致志。
整日里，他的话题不离时间，

All day we felt and watched the sun
Caged in its white diurnal heat,
Pointing at us with its black stick.

整日里，我们体察那轮白日，
而它被围裹在白昼的炽热中，
正用一条黑鞭挥向我们。

Foghorns

When Catrin was a small child
She thought the foghorn moaning
Far out at sea was the sad
Solitary voice of the moon
Journeying to England.
She heard it warn "Moon, Moon,"
As it worked the Channel, trading
Weather like rags and bones.

Tonight, after the still sun
And the silent heat, as haze
Became rain and weighed glistening

雾角

凯特琳年少时
以为远海雾角吹出
的哀鸣声似一轮明月
在前往英格兰时
所发出的悲声孤鸣。
她闻见了"脉，脉"①的警鸣声，
原来是雾角吹响整个海峡，正营运
天气，如旧衣残骨②。

今晚夕阳西下，
天气沉闷，烟雾
成雨，在繁枝茂叶中

---

① 脉，脉的英文原诗是 moon, moon，双关语，既指月亮，又是拟声词，因发音与雾角声一样，故女孩联想到月亮。"脉"字因月字旁，自然而然联想到与月相关，有声有象，与原诗词 moon 的功能吻合。李贺《九月》中诗句"月缀金铺光脉脉"便是旁证。——译者注
② 英文原诗中 rags and bones，源自文化负载词 rag and bone。它指的是以前英国威尔士农村，经常有收破烂的"商人"或乞丐等挨家挨户去收买破旧废物，如旧衣服，残羹中牛、羊、鸡等骨头。英文原诗中的 trade weather，源自化用的 trade wind，根据牛津英语字典词条解释，该短语指大风不断朝一个方向，延续时间长，通常发生在海域上，尤其让人联想到季风性气候的印度洋海域和热带的东风气候。此处诗人化海风为海雾天气，重在暗示雾之跨度大、时间长。——译者注

In brimful leaves, and the last bus
Splashes and fades with a soft
Wave-sound, the foghorns moan, moon—
Lonely and the dry lawns drink.
This dimmed moon, calling still,
Hauls sea-rags through the streets.

金光闪烁，最后一趟汽车
激起水花后，随着一声柔波
消逝，雾角孤吟，脉——
草地干燥，吞饮雨水。
雾角的低鸣声依旧，
拖着海布满街奔走。

Storm Awst

The cat walks. It listens, as I do,
To the wind which leans its iron
Shoulders on our door. Neither
The purr of a cat nor my blood
Runs smoothly for elemental fear
Of the storm. This then is the big weather
They said was coming. All the signs
Were bad, the gulls coming in white,
Lapwings gathering, the sheep too
Calling all night. The gypsies
Were making their fires in the woods
Down there in the east... always
A warning. The rain stings, the whips
Of the laburnum hedge lash the roof
Of the cringing cottage. A curious
Calm, coming from the storm, unites
Us, as we wonder if the work
We have done will stand. Will the tyddyn
In its group of strong trees on the high

八月暴风雨

猫在行走。它如我一般侧耳倾听
风声，而风的一件件铁
肩则压在我们的房门上。猫
那惬意的呼噜声和我的血液
皆因惧怕暴风雨而无法
畅行。这便是他们所预言的
将临的恶劣天气。所有迹象
皆为凶相：海鸥白茫茫一片地飞来，
田凫围拢积聚，羊群也在
彻夜咩咩喊叫。一群吉卜赛人
则在那东边的林地里
生起篝火……历来
视为一种警报。雨滴如刺，金链花
树篱那一次次挥鞭抽打着
畏缩的房顶。一种奇妙
的冷静，因暴雨所致，让我们
齐心共济，欲知所做之事
能否存续。八月的暴风雨[①]
席卷这座高丘时，万物竖耳聆听，

_____

① 在英文原诗中，诗人用威尔士语 Awst 来指代"八月"，并在诗歌末尾给出英文对应词 August。——译者注

Hill, hold against the storm Awst
Running across hills where everything
Alive listens, pacing its house, heart still?

storm Awst: August storm
tyddyn: smallholding

临渊测步，却心安神泰，

而此处小农场^①，为坚卓之林所环抱，

能否不畏风雨，坚韧屹立？

---

① 在英文原诗中，诗人用威尔士语 tyddyn 来指代"小农场"，并在诗歌末尾给出英文对应词 smallholding。——译者注

Last Rites

During this summer of the long drought
The road to Synod Inn has kept
Its stigmata of dust and barley seed;

At the inquest they tell it again:
How the lorry tents us from the sun,
His pulse dangerous in my hands,
A mains hum only, no message
Coming through. His face warm, profiled
Against tarmac, the two-stoke Yamaha
Dead as a black horse in a war.
Only his hair moves and the sound
Of the parched grass and harebells a handspan
Away, his fear still with me like the scream
Of a jet in an empty sky.
I cover him with the grey blanket
From my bed, touch his face as a child

最后的仪式

这个夏天正逢一场久旱，
通往西诺德客栈^①的道路留有
粉尘和麦粒的圣痕；

询问时他们再度告知：
货车如何为人们遮阴蔽日，
他的脉搏在我的双手中危在旦夕，
唯有主线路的嗡嗡声，无任何讯息
传来。他那温润的脸庞贴在
柏油路面，而那辆两缸的雅马哈^②
则像一匹战死沙场的黑马。
唯有他的头发在飘动，一只手
的距离外，枯草和风信子沙沙
作响，而他的恐惧依旧伴我左右，若喷气式飞机
在辽阔的天空中发出的轰鸣声。
我从床上拿起那条灰色的毛毯
盖在他的身上，抚摸着他的脸，犹如女孩儿

---

① 西诺德客栈（Synod Inn）既是客栈名，也是客栈所在的村庄名，位于威尔士达费德郡，靠近西海岸卡迪根湾（Cardigan Bay），离斯旺西西北部 41 英里（1 英里约等于 1.61 千米）。——译者注
② 雅马哈是一家日企，既经营钢琴、木管、大小提琴等乐器，又涉足摩托车、发动机等汽车领域的产品。此处诗人意指摩托车。——译者注

15

Who makes her favourites cosy.
His blood on my hands, his cariad in my arms.

Driving her home we share that vision
Over August fields dying of drought
Of the summer seas shattering
At every turn of Cardigan Bay
Under the cruel stones of the sun.

爱抚自己的心爱之物。
我的双手沾满了他的鲜血，怀里温存着他的挚爱。

驱车送她回家途中，我们共享一片景致：
越过因酷旱而凋敝的八月原野，
远处那面炎夏海域，
在严酷的骄阳灼石下，支离破碎，
每当绕过卡迪根湾之时。

At One Thousand Feet

Nobody comes but the postman
and the farmer with winter fodder.

A-road and motorway avoid me.
The national grid has left me out.

For power I catch wind.
In my garden clear water rises.

A wind spinning the blades
of the mill to blinding silver

lets in the rumour,
grief on the radio.

America telephones.
A postcard comes from Poland.

In the sling of its speed the comet
flowers to perihelion over the chimney.

I hold the sky to my ear to hear
pandemonium whispering.

千步之遥

无人来此，除了邮递员
和备着过冬草料的农夫。

A 级公路、摩托车道避开我。
国家电网已将我抛弃。

为了力量，我抓住风。
花园之中，清水上涨。

风旋转着磨坊
风车叶片闪烁着耀眼的银色，

迎进流言蜚语，
收音机放着哀乐。

美国来电。
一张来自波兰的明信片。

彗星飞速掠过，在烟囱上方，
近日点处，如花绽放。

我将天空凑近耳朵
聆听喧嚣窃窃私语。

Windmill

On the stillest day
not enough breath to rock the hedge
it smashes the low sun to smithereens.

Quicker than branch to find a thread of air
that'll tow a gale off the Atlantic
by way of Lundy, Irish Sea.

At night it knocks stars from their perches
and casts a rhythmic beating of the moon
into my room in bright blades.

It kneels into the wind-race
and slaps black air to foam.
Helping to lower and lift it again

I feel it thrash in dark water
drumming with winds from the Americas
to run through my fingers' circle

holding the earth's breath.

风坊

在至静至寂的日子里，
气息不足以撼动篱笆，
它将低阳碾成粉碎。

它比树枝更敏锐地察觉到气流，
在途经蓝迪岛、爱尔兰海时，
将拖住大西洋的狂风。

夜幕降临，它敲醒沉睡的繁星，
用明亮的风叶将皓月
所奏响的旋律送至我的房间。

它屈跪于疾风之中，
将黑气拍打成泡沫。
助它时降时升，

只见它猛拍着黑水，
声如鼓，伴随美洲吹来的狂风
穿梭在我的指圈中，

屏住大地的气息。

A Photograph from Space

Fluorescence hums overhead
and town after town winks
along the curve of the bay.

From far out in the dark
the map is luminous.
Our jewels gleam,
North America, Europe
drawn in light,

while Africa is a dark house,
India missing from the photograph,
relatives no one remembered to call
for the family picture.

一张太空航拍照

头顶上方的荧光嗡嗡作响，
顺着海湾的曲线，眨眼
闪烁地飘过每一座城镇。

远眺深邃的黑暗中，
地图发出耀眼的光芒。
一枚枚微亮的珠宝——
北美洲、欧洲——
由光线所勾勒。

而非洲俨然一栋幽暗之屋，
照片中也难觅印度的踪影，
亲友之间也无人惦记相约
来拍一张全家福。

Valley

after glass and slate sculpture by Meical Watts

In water-memory the river turns
always the same way at the boulder
and the bridge.
An ess of current at the land's shoulder,
the falling back of a sleeve where light burns
otter silk below the ridge.

A million million years of water-work
to make this place. A whispering seepage
through lion grass on fire
under snow. A stream's gleaming back
lifts from the mist and marshy weep
as flood meets deep and secret aquifers.

山谷

观看麦卡尔·沃茨 [①] 的玻璃雕塑与板岩雕塑后有感而作

水的记忆里，这条河总是
以相同的方式在巨砾
和桥梁处拐弯。
陆地肩头处一股 S 形湍流，
仿若一袭长袖的回落，而山脊之下
燃着一束水獭般丝柔鲜亮的光。

上百万年的水工之力
才造就了此地。潺潺的流水
透过火红的狮子草
渗入雪下。一条溪流的闪烁背影
从轻雾和沼泽的呜咽中升腾，
而洪流则与深隐的地下含水层交融汇合。

[①] 麦卡尔·沃茨（Meical Watts）生于 1962 年，当代英国威尔士艺术家、画家和雕塑家，曾于二十世纪八十年代初在诺里奇艺术学院学习美术，在诸多国家和地区，比如英格兰、威尔士和美国，举办过个人作品展，诸多作品被私人和机构收藏。他以威尔士著名的矿石原料板岩和石头进行雕刻作画，反映威尔士的风土人情，其作品深受广大威尔士人的喜爱。——译者注

Dwyfor and Glaslyn, green-black rivers of the north
tumbling boulders for the walls of farms,
slip chisels of glass between the slate.
A rumour of ice, flood-fingers in sodden earth.
The bell of an old glacier in the rock's seams
so it splits clean at a tap of light.

Weather works the mountain to the bone
with the let juices of rain, the rising sea's erosion,
a river's gravity, flood's cold reflection,
a valley cut by water over stone.

德威弗尔 ① 和格拉斯林 ②，两条北方青黛河流，
翻腾在砌农场围墙之用的巨砾之间，
流转在板岩间那把把玻璃錾凿之中。
那是冰的传言，似洪流的根根手指插入泥地之中，
而岩缝中响起了一道道古老冰川的钟声，
它，在光的轻触下，坼裂离析。

气候刻骨镂心地演化着此处山脉：
雨水周期性的淋淫、海水上升时的侵蚀、
河流的重力、洪水的寒气回溯，
而石上的流水则不断切割山谷。

---

① 德威弗尔（Dwyfor）即 Afon Dwyfor，意为两（Dwy）海（for）之间的
河流（afon），位于北威尔士丽茵半岛（Llŷn Peninsula）克里基厄斯镇
（Criccieth）附近。——译者注
② 格拉斯林（Glaslyn）在威尔士语中，意为蓝湖，流淌于威尔士中部腹
地坎布里安山脉（Cambrian Mountains）之间。——译者注

Advent

After the wideawake galaxies
each dawn is glass.
Leavings of the night's kill lie,
twig-bones, ice-feathers,
the ghost of starlight.

Ewes breathe silver.
The rose won't come—
stopped in her tracks.
Everything's particular:
bramble's freehand,

a leaf caught out,
the lawn's journal.
Deep down even the water-table
stiffens its linen,
and horizons pleat in a bucket.

The stars burn out
to starved birds
watching my window,
and one leaf puts up a hand
against infinite light.

降临

星系清醒湛明之后，
黎明即镜。
夜晚的杀戮残迹犹存：
枝如骨，冰若羽，
星光恰似幽灵。

母羊嘘噙着银光。
玫瑰不会盛开——
却在途中逗留。
万物卓诡不伦：
荆棘随手而作，

树叶已被揭露，
化作草坪的日志。
甚至地下深处水位的表面
僵硬得如一块亚麻布，
而地平线在水桶中起皱。

繁星燃尽，
面朝饥肠辘辘的鸟儿，
遥望我的窗台，
而一片树叶抬手
遮蔽了永恒之光。

Flood

When all's said
and done
if civilisation drowns
the last colour to go
will be gold
the light on a glass,
the prow of a gondola,
the name on a rosewood piano
as silence engulfs it,

and first to return
to a waterlogged world,
the rivers slipping out to sea,
the cities steaming,
will be gold,
one dip from Bellini's brush,
feathers of angels,
Cinquecento nativities,
and all that follows.

洪荒

尘埃（该说的都说了）
落定（该做的都做了）：
倘若文明湮没，
最后消逝的颜色
便是金色，
就像玻璃杯上的光泽、
贡多拉凤尾船的船首色、
檀木钢琴上的签名色，
当宁静吞没它时，

而最先重返的，
回到一个水涝的世界，
似涓涓细流汇入的大川，
一座座热气腾腾的都市，
也将是金色，
就像贝利尼①画笔下的一滴颜料、
天使的羽毛、
十六世纪意大利的文艺叙事，
以及此后的万物众生。

---

① 贝利尼即意大利著名威尼斯画派画家乔凡尼·贝利尼（Giovanni Bellini，1430—1516）。——译者注

Water Resources

水资源

Syphoning the Spring

We have struggled all day to syphon water.

This morning, the air blue and the damp,
the wet, the glitter of water rose
through our fingers from a hose
dipped into drilled rock.
But the hose isn't long enough nor the hill
steep enough for water to come.
For an hour it falters in the bed of the stream
among wild forgetmenots, tracing water-veins
with their hint of mist, of water-breath.
Then we bind the pump to the hose again
and pump and pump till the bubble of rubber fills
with certain water, then drive the handle down.

Through flared fingers the water comes
like birth-water, catching green light
of fern and cresses and blue forgetmenots.

While we are sleeping
water moves in moonlight,
a slow pulse in the shallows.

抽吸山泉

我们整日都在奋力抽水。

今早，蔚蓝的天空下，只见
水管中水流升起，潮气和湿气涌现，
波光粼粼，水透过指间，
滴入岩石的钻孔之中。
然而，抽水胶管的长度短了些，山坡
的斜度也不够陡，水无法涌出。
它在河床里蹒跚了一个小时，
在野生的忘忧草间，顺着丝丝雾气，
倾听水的气息，探寻水脉。
不久，我们再度将水泵绑在水管上，
连续抽吸，直至胶管中盛了
些水，而后我们才将手柄向下压。

通过通红的双手，泉水冒出
如羊水一般，捎带蕨类植物、
水芹和蓝色忘忧草所泛起的青光。

我们入眠之际，
水波在月光中浮动，
浅浅泉水，涓涓细流。

Some time in the night it will stop,
in the dead hour when people die,
till we borrow more hose, find a steeper hill
so that it dares to fall clear, for it wants
to fall, to give itself, knowing the risk.

或许，午夜时分，水流停歇，
恰逢在有人离世的紧要关头，
直到我们去借更多的水管，寻找更陡的山坡，
如此，泉水便能畅流而下，因为它想
降落，奉献自己，虽然明知其中的风险。

Rain

A light across the garden through the rain
that silks itself all day into the earth,
through porous shale into the aquifers,
deeper and deeper finding its way to bedrock.

A light through the smoke of rain from the barn
where he strokes curls of wood through the mouth of the plane,
shaving the sap-rings where the tree once drank
its prodigious sips of old deep water.

We'll both think, "who are you?", when he comes in
through the falling rain and we stand in the light of a room
seeing each other strange again after nothing
but seas breaking between the continents.

His hands will be sappy with sycamore, oak or pine,
whatever he's been easing through oiled steel,
familiar as rain, the tools, and pages. The house
will reclaim us, offering firelight, music, a glass of wine,

after the rain and the oceans between us, grace,
landfall, the communion of a gaze.

雨

一束光穿过雨幕，在花园里穿梭，
整日犹如丝线穿入大地，
透过多孔的页岩渗入含水层，
越流越深，直抵基岩。

一束光穿透从谷仓落下的雨雾，
谷仓中，他用刨子刨平木材的卷曲处，
刨光木头上的树液轮，那是这棵树曾经
啜饮古老深水的奇妙印记。

当他冒着淅淅沥沥的雨进来时，我们彼此会
心生疑惑："尊驾谓谁？"而后伫立，借着屋里的灯光
再次面面相觑，互感陌生，唯见
身后横在大陆之间那片惊涛拍岸的汪洋大海。

他的双手或许沾满梧桐树、橡树或松树的汁液，
无论他刚刚用油涂过的刨刀刨平过何物，
一切熟悉如雨、工具和书页。这座房子
将改造我们，给予我们炉火、音乐和一杯红酒，

雨停后，跨越我俩之间的大洋之后，恩典降临，
我们靠岸着陆，相互凝视，会心一笑。

Ice

Where beech cast off her clothes
frost has got its knives out.

This is the chemistry of ice,
the stitchwork, the embroidery,
the froth and the flummery.

Light joins in. It has a point to make
about haloes and glories,
spectra and reflection.

It reflects on its own miracle,
the first imagined day
when the dark was blown

and there was light.

冰

山毛榉脱下她的外衣时，
冰霜亮出了把把尖刀。

这是冰的魔力，
时而像一幅刺绣，一件装饰品，
时而又像一堆泡沫，一个冻状物。

光加了进来。它有自己的诠释，
对于光环和光荣，
对于光谱和反射。

它以独特的魅力反射
那想象中的首日：
黑暗消散，

曙光降临。

Flora and Landscape

植物与景观

Snow on the Mountain

There was a girl riding a white pony
Which seemed an elemental part
Of the snow. A crow cut a clean line
Across the hill, which we grasped as a rope
To pull us up the pale diagonal.

The point was to be first at the top
Of the mountain. Our laughter bounced far
Below us like five fists full of pebbles. About us
Lay the snow, deep in the hollows,
Very clean and dry, untouched.

I arrived breathless, my head breaking
The surface of the glittering light, thinking
No place could claim more beauty, white
Slag tips like cones of sugar spun
By the pit wheels under Machen mountain.

I sat on a rock in the sun, watching
My snowboys play. Pit villages shine

雪山

有位女孩儿骑着一匹小白马，
不知不觉成了雪中一道亮丽
的风景线。一只乌鸦掠过山坡，划出
一条清晰的线，我们抓着它，仿佛一根绳索
拽着我们顺着皓白的对角线向上爬。

关键是要做到登顶
第一。我们载欢载笑，声音远下
回荡，似五个握满鹅卵石的拳头。环顾四周，
茫茫的积雪，深藏于坳洼之中，
洁净如玉，纤尘不染。

到达时我已气喘吁吁，头顶划破了
那灿烂夺目的光面，默叹
此处风景独好，而白色
的矿渣尖堆犹如玛阡山 [①] 下
那一台台矿井机轮纺出的糖锥。

阳光下我坐在岩石上，望着
我的雪娃在嬉戏。一座座矿区村落发出

---

① 玛阡山的英文是 Machen Mountain 或 Machen Hill，位于英国威尔士南部。——译者注

Like anthracite. Completed, the pale rider
Rode away. I turned to him, and saw
His joy fall like the laughter down a dark
Crack. The black crow shadowed him.

无烟煤般的光亮。事毕，一位苍白的骑者
乘马而去。我转身望向他，只见
他的欢声笑语顺着一道幽暗的裂缝
降落。而那只乌鸦则与他如影随形。

Beech Buds

The beech buds are breaking. I feel so happy.
I snapped the bare twigs in a wood
A month ago. I put them in a wine bottle
Filled with water, not for the twigs, for the light
Blown bubbles to float in the shine of the water.

It was like that with my life. I put
Something that was dead and bare into
The brightness of your love, not so that
Leaf would break, but for the bubbles
Of silver against the light. From the hard,
Brittle wood came tenderness and life, numerous
Damp, green butterflies, transparently veined,
Opening like a tree that is alive.

山毛榉新芽

山毛榉正吐露新芽，我顿时喜上眉梢。
一个月前，我猛然摘下林中一些
光秃秃的枝条，而后将它们放入一个盛满水
的酒瓶里，并非为了枝条本身，而是为了
轻盈的气泡能悬浮在水的光辉中。

人生莫过如此。我将
枯萎、光秃之物放入
您心爱的光亮中，并非期望
叶不凋零，而是期盼银色
的气泡映照着光明。脆木历经枯硬
便迎来柔嫩和生命，而无数
潮润的绿蝶，带着晶莹的纹络，
展翅飞舞，仿若焕发蓬勃生机的树木。

Plums

When their time comes they fall
without wind, without rain.
They seep through the trees' muslin
in a slow fermentation.

Daily the low sun warms them
in a late love that is sweeter
than summer. In bed at night
we hear heartbeat of fruitfall.

The secretive slugs crawl home
to the burst honeys, are found
in the morning mouth on mouth,
inseparable.

We spread patchwork counterpanes
for a clean catch. Baskets fill,
never before such harvest,
such a hunters' moon burning

李子

成熟时，它们自然坠落，
无风，也无雨。
它们在缓慢发酵，
透过李树的薄纱逐渐渗出浆汁。

微弱的阳光日日暖和着它们，
犹如一份晚至的爱，相比夏天
显得愈加的美好。夜晚躺在床上时，
我们便能听到果实落下的心跳声。

一只只隐蔽的蛞蝓爬回
香蜜充盈的家中，次日
清晨，却被发现嘴嘴相连，
难以分离。

我们将一张张拼缀的床单铺开，
以便收获洁净的果子。篮筐满满，
如此的丰收景象，未曾见过，
恰似一轮猎人之月 ① 燃烧着

---

① 猎人之月又叫狩猎月，即十月份最接近秋分时狩猎丰收的满月，一般
在 10 月 20 日。——译者注

the hawthorns, drunk on syrups
that are richer by night
when spiders are pitching
tents in the wet grass.

This morning the red sun
is opening like a rose
on our white wall, prints there
the fishbone shadow of a fern.

The early blackbirds fly
guilty from a dawn haul
of fallen fruit. We too
breakfast on sweetnesses.

Soon plum trees will be bone,
grown delicate with frost's
formalities. Their black
angles will tear the snow.

山楂树，饮着糖浆，
而每当夜晚蜘蛛
在湿草中搭起帐篷之时，
糖浆便愈加地芬芳。

今日清晨，一轮红日
如玫瑰花般怒放
在我们的白壁上，留下了
一株蕨类植物的鱼骨状影子。

黎明时分，夙起的乌鸫
从落果间飞来，
惭愧不已。我们同样
吃着早餐，以香李为食。

不久，株株李树傲霜
斗雪，瘦骨嶙峋，
而它们漆黑的棱角
终将积雪扯攞，让其陨泣。

All Souls' Night

Wind after rain. The lane
is beaten lead. Nothing

is any colour. Hedges
are scribbles of darkness.

Not a cow or sheep in grey fields.
Rain sings in the culverts,

slides the gate-bars, brambles and grasses,
glints in tyre-ruts and hoof-prints.

Only the springer's fur flowers white,
will o' the wisp under a gate

across a field short-sightedly
reading the script of the fox.

A sudden wheel of starlings turns
the hill's corner, their wings a whish

of air, the darkening sound

万灵之夜

雨后风起。道路
被鞭打成铅块。万物

毫无色彩。树篱
像极了黑暗的涂绘。

原野灰暗,不见牛羊。
雨在暗渠中吟唱,

溜过门杆、刺藤和草丛,
在车辙和蹄印中闪耀。

唯有獴狗的软毛如花绽白,
鬼火般在门下随风飞舞,

越过原野,短视地
盯着狐狸的足迹。

突然,一群椋鸟盘旋飞过
山角,羽翼在空中呼呼

作响,仿佛暗影掠过

of a shadow crossing land.

At a touch my bare ash tree rings,
leafed, shaken,

the stopper of ice dissolved
in each bird-throat,

the frozen ash
become a burning bush.

大地所发出的声音。

我那裸露的白蜡树一触即应，
叶叶被翻阅，枝枝被摇晃，

驻足的冰雪消融
在每只椋鸟的歌喉中，

而冰封的灰烬
化作丛丛炽烈的荆棘。

Nettles

for Edward Thomas

No old machinery, no tangled chains
of a harrow locked in rust and rising grasses,
nor the fallen stones of ancient habitation
where nettles feed on what we leave behind.
Nothing but a careless compost heap
warmed to a simmer of sickly pungency,
lawn clippings we never moved, but meant to,

and can't, now, because nettles have moved in,
and it's your human words inhabit this.
And, closer, look! The stems lean with the weight,
the young of peacock butterflies, just hatched,
their glittering black spines and spots of pearl.
And I want to say to the dead, look what a poet sings
to life: the bite of nettles, caterpillars, wings.

荨麻

致敬爱德华·托马斯

此处古址不见废旧的机械，不见
铁齿交缠锈蚀的钉耙和滋长的荒草，
亦无房屋倒塌的石块，却滋生着
依赖人类所弃之物为生的<u>丛丛</u>荨麻。
别无他物唯见一处凌乱的堆肥
升温沸腾，直至散发出恶心的刺鼻味儿，
尽是些本应移走却未曾移走的草屑，

如今更不可能移走，因为荨麻早已入住，
而且人类的语言也依附其中。
走近，细瞧！荨麻茎秆因负重而倾斜，
而一只只孔雀蝶幼虫，刚孵化破卵而出，
身带珍珠般璀璨夺目的黑脊和斑驳。
我想对逝者诉说，聆听诗人如何歌颂
生命：荨麻之蜇、蝴蝎之咬、蝶翼之寒。

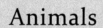

Animals

动物

Sheep's Skulls

The bone is thin as paper
Inside the skull, scrolled on shadow.
Its dreams evaporated
On a warm bank over the drover's road
To Capel Cynon.

We sought skulls like mushrooms,
Uncertainly white at a distance,
Skulls of sheep, rabbit, bird,
Beautiful as a leaf's skeleton
Or derelict shell,

Where sheep shelter inside stone
Cottages, graze the floors clean, stare
From the window spaces. They die
On the open hill, and raven and buzzard
Come like women to clean them.

The skull's caves are secretive.
The crazed bone, sometimes translucent
As vellum, sometimes shawled
To lace, no longer knocks with the heart's bell

羊颅骨

头颅之内，骨头
薄如纸片，卷影重重。
它的梦想在暖堤上
蒸发，飘过牲畜贩子的路
奔赴凯农教堂。

我们寻找颅骨，如同寻找蘑菇，
远望隐约白茫茫一片：
羊颅骨、兔颅骨、鸟颅骨，
美得像极了树叶的轮廓，
或遗弃的贝壳，

而羊群在石屋内歇息，
将地上的草吃得精光，
透过窗户向外凝视。它们死
在开阔的山坡上，渡鸦和秃鹰
则像女人一样前来清理。

颅骨的洞穴通常隐蔽。
龟裂的骨头，时而牛皮纸般
微微透亮，时而像裹着
一层蕾丝，不再为腹中

To the lamb in the womb.

A spider wraps it in a tress
Of silk, a cloth of light. On the rose
Patina of old wood it lies
Ornamental in the reflection
Of a jar of wheat stalks.

的羔羊敲响心钟。

一只蜘蛛用长长的丝线将它
缠绕，犹如一块光布。在古木
的玫瑰斑驳上，它躺在
一坛麦秆的斜影之中，
仿若一件装饰品。

Curlews

We crouched in the wet field, gambling
Numb hours for the prize of a curlew's
Nest. The pair fussed in the sky, diving
To run in the lost lanes of the grass.

We heard the young call close to us
In small mimicry of adult
Panic, flecked, soft spheres on long,
Grey legs, following the sky's signal.

We held one, folded and frail, beak
Minutely curved, freckled like a blown,
Pale dandelion. Then it ran, free,
Into the secret homeward corridors.

Our important morning had given
Its joy. Then we turned to go home
And found the broken baby curlew,
Death glazing its black eyes with pain.

Inconsolably we watched the head
Loll from the snapped stem of its neck

杓鹬

我们蹲伏在湿漉漉的野地上，赌上
沉滞的时光，以获取杓鹬巢穴中
的奖励。一对杓鹬在空中惊慌失措，俯冲
扑向草丛的幽径中，迷失了方向。

我们听见幼雏在不远处
轻声模仿成鸟的鸣叫，
神情恐慌，身上斑纹点点，柔软的球体下
长着一双灰色的长腿，追寻空中的讯号。

我们手握其中一只，它屈卧着，脆弱无力，鸟喙
微微弧起，带着斑点，犹如一朵被风吹过
苍白的蒲公英。不久，它跑了，自由
钻进那条条通往家园的密道。

美好的清晨赋予了我们
以欢乐。之后，当转身启程回家时，
我们却发现那只伤残的幼雏，
死神用痛楚让它那双鸟亮的眼睛渐渐呆滞。

望着它的头从被掐断的脖颈上
垂了下来，宛如一朵蒲公英的挂钟

Like the hung clock of a dandelion
Wasting its seed. We grieved to see.

Time fall, life by life, no comfort to give
To each other. Did we crush it
As we passed, greedy as hunters
To possess the summer's wildness?

在消耗自己的种子，我们一筹莫展，
悲痛欲绝，不忍直视。

万物生机逝如斯，彼辈慰藉
难相寄。当我们经过时，
是否像猎户那样贪图
夏日的狂野不羁而不惜将它碾碎？

Choughs

I follow you downhill to the edge
My feet taking as naturally as yours
To a sideways tread, finding footholds
Easily in the turf, accustomed
As we are to a sloping country.

The cliffs buttress the bay's curve to the north
And here drop sheer and sudden to the sea.
The choughs plummet from sight then ride
The updraught of the cliffs' mild yellow
Light, fold, fall with closed wings from the sky.

At the last moment as in unison they turn
A ripcord of the wind is pulled in time.
He gives her food and the saliva
Of his red mouth, draws her black feathers, sweet
As shining grass across his bill.

Rare birds that pair for life. There they go
Divebombing the marbled wave a yard
Above the spray. Wings flick open
A stoop away
From the drawn teeth of the sea.

山鸦

我随你们下山来到山的边缘，
双脚像你们的一样自然地
侧着踩，发现轻轻松松地
在草地上找到立足点，正如
我们惯于行走在有坡度的地方。

那悬崖峭壁朝北托起了海湾的弧线，
在此处陡然坠入海中。
一只只山鸦从眼前骤然跃下，而后乘着
崖壁那股柔和的、带着黄光的上升
气流，曲折躯干，收起羽翼，从天而降。

最后时刻，他们整齐划一地转身，
及时拉开了风的开伞索。
他从自己的红嘴中给她喂食，
给她唾液，用喙将她的根根黑羽梳得楚楚动人，
犹如株株晶莹亮丽的嫩草。

珍稀鸟类，相伴终生。他们相约
在水花溅起一英码① 高的大理石花纹般的波浪上
俯冲猛击。双翼轻轻弹开，
一个躬身，飞离
海上那排苍白的利齿。

---

① 1 码等于 3 英尺，约等于 0.914 米。——译者注

A Dream of Horses

I dreamed a gallop across sand
in and out the scallop of the tide
on a colourless horse as cold as a seal.

My hair and the mane of the horse
are the long white manes of the sea.
Every breath is a gulp of salt.

Now we are ocean. His hoof-prints
are pools, his quivering skin
the silk in the trough of the wave.

His muscular ellipses are
the sinuous long water of the sea
and I swim with the waves in my arms.

梦马

我梦见自己驾着一匹无色骏马，
冷若海豹，驰骋于沙地之上，
进出于潮水的扇形边缘。

我的头发和那匹骏马的鬃毛
化作大海那又长又密的白发。
每一次呼吸如同吞咽一口白盐。

如今，我们便是大海。他的蹄印
宛若湾湾池塘，而抖动的皮肤
仿若浪谷中的丝绸。

他那椭圆形的壮健肌肉酷似
迤逦悠长的海水，
而我张开双臂，随浪遨游。

Spaniel

Between the two of us
everything is more.
About the stern commands—
fetch, lie, stay—
or the clear images—
ball, stick, bed—
are the qualifying clauses,
muscular syntax
that helps me think aloud.
My voice speaks what her tongue,
tail, racing feet say too.
Across the fields she runs
nose down to the sinuous
language of smell
telling the secret
inbetween things of speech.

Together we find a hare
killed on the road.
She knows its nightly track,
its way of death, who plundered it
and where, on paws, on wings they fled.

猎狗

你我之间更多
是互相信赖。
涉及严肃的命令——
取、躺、站——
抑或明晰的意象——
球、棍、床——
皆是达标的修饰从句，
健硕的句法，
助我大声说出自己的想法。
我的声音也诉说着她的舌头、
尾巴和矫健步伐所传达之意。
她驰骋原野，
鼻子嗅到气味
那柔美迂回的语言，
像在吐露言语
之间的秘密。

我们共同发现一只野兔
在马路上死于非命。
她知晓它的夜行足迹
和死亡方式，明了谁剥夺了它的性命，
也清楚他们爬行或飞行逃至何处。

While she is wild and trembles
with the night's history,
I am stilled by its myth.
With my boot I gently
roll the dead hare
to the dignity of the ditch.
Because she thinks I am wise
she is silent, still, wide-eyed.

当她因昨夜的历史

而发狂战栗时，

我却因昨夜的神话而沉着冷静。

我用靴子将毙命的野兔

轻轻地滚入沟渠，

一个有尊严的安息地。

她觉得我聪明伶俐，

故默不作声，纹丝不动，虎目圆睁。

Swimming with Seals

Two horizons:
a far blue where a ship
diminishes and the evening sun
lets slip;
and submarine
where we glimpse stars and shoals
and shadowy water-gardens
of what's beyond us.

When the seal rises
she rests her chin on the sea
as we do, and tames us with her gaze.
On shore the elderly
bask beside their cars
at the edge of what they've lost,
and shade their eyes
and lift binoculars.

She's gone,
apt to the sea's grace
to watch us underwater from her place,
you with your mask and fins,

与海豹共游

两条地平线：
远方一线蓝，一艘轮船
渐渐变小，一轮夕阳
滑落；
水下一线蓝，
我们瞥见繁星、鱼群，
以及环绕四周
那幽暗的水花园。

当海豹浮起时，
她的下巴像我们一样
歇在海面上，用凝视折服我们。
沙滩上的老人们
在车旁所消失的边缘处，
享受日光浴，
遮着双眼，
举着望远镜。

她离开了，
习惯性地游向大海的优雅处，
从所处的位置观察水下的我们：
你戴着面具和鳍，

strolling the shallow gardens of the sea,
me, finding depth
with a child's flounder of limbs,
hauling downwards on our chains of breath.

For a moment the old
looking out to sea,
all earth's weight beneath their folding chairs,
see only flawless blue to the horizon,
while we in seconds of caught air,
swim down against buoyancy,
rolling in amnion
like her September calf.

来回徜徉在海下的浅水花园；
而我，像一位极力挣扎四肢
的孩童，探寻深处，
在生命的呼吸链上往下拽。

此刻，老人们
望向大海，
大地的重量在他们的折叠椅下方，
他们只见到海平面上那完美的蓝域，
而我们凭借短暂的屏气，
不顾浮力向下游，
翻腾在羊膜中，
宛然她九月出生的幼崽。

Fulmarus Glacialis

for Christine Evans

Filing the fulmar you post me from Llŷn
I turn to the bird-book and the cliffs.

Found first in Iceland, 1750,
glacial bird whose wings of snow
throw images of angels on the sea
or a gutfull of stinking oil in the enemy's face.

Pilgrim. Discovever. On the bird-map
Britain's little island's coiffed
with foam of fulmar.
Once rare visitor, she takes the coast.

Between small-print of shore
and broad stroke of the littoral
is fulmar territory, Rockall to Fastnet,
Lundy to Hebrides.

In seabird's slow increase she drew the map
in feathery sea-script, set her single egg

暴风鹱

致克里斯蒂娜·埃文斯

整理好您从丽茵半岛寄来的暴风鹱，
我开始翻阅鸟类书籍，前往崖壁观察。

此类冰川鸟于 1750 年
首次在冰岛被发现，其雪白的羽翼
使人想到海上的天使，
抑或敌人满脸的臭油。

它是朝圣者、发现者。依鸟类分布图所示，
大不列颠群岛的小岛戴着
一圈暴风鹱的泡沫。
曾为稀客，现如今它却占领了各大海岸。

从罗科尔到法斯特耐特，
从伦迪到赫布里底群岛，
在狭窄和宽阔的海岸线之间，
皆是暴风鹱的领地。

在物种缓慢繁衍的进程中，它用羽状的大海文字
绘制了一幅地图，并在每一座岩架

on the palm of every ledge
till that first visitor became a million birds.

Bridle the fulmar. Borrow the lover's llatai
for carrying a message to a friend
a hundred miles or so across the Bay
down the bright water-lines, Ceredigion to Llŷn.

的掌心上产下一枚蛋，
直到初客繁衍出无数的后代。

降伏其中一只。借来挚爱的"爱情信使"，
让它从锡尔迪金郡沿着明亮的海岸线，
跨越一百多英里的海湾，飞抵丽茵半岛，
给远方的朋友捎去一个口信。

Mineral Ecology

矿物生态

Journey

As far as I am concerned
We are driving into oblivion.
On either side there is nothing,
And beyond your driving
Shaft of light it is black.
You are a miner digging
For a future, a mineral
Relationship in the dark.
I can hear the darkness drip
From the other world where people
Might be sleeping, might be alive.

Certainly there are white
Gates with churns waiting
For morning, their cream standing.
Once we saw an old table
Standing square on the grass verge.
Our lamps swept it clean, shook
The crumbs into the hedge and left it.
A tractor too, beside a load
Of logs, bringing from a deeper
Dark a damp whiff of the fungoid

旅行

依我之见，
我们将驶入遗忘之境。
境里境外一无所有。
驶过光明之轴
坠入黑暗之境。
你是一名矿工挖向
未来，黑暗中
与矿物建立关系。
我隐约听见黑暗
从另一世界滴落，那里人们
或睡，或醒，或活着。

当然彼岸屹立白色
大门，搅乳桶等待
清晨，桶内乳脂伫立。
我们曾见一张旧桌
四四方方，立在草边。
灯光将其扫净，抖落
面包屑于树篱中，然后离开。
还有辆卡车，柴火堆旁，
从更深阴暗处
带回一股潮湿，布满真菌，

Sterility of the conifers.

Complacently I sit, swathed
In sleepiness. A door shuts
At the end of a dark corridor.
Ahead not a cat's eye winks
To deceive us with its green
Invitation. As you hurl us
Into the black contracting
Chasm, I submit like a blind
And folded baby, being born.

针叶枯萎的气味。

我洋洋得意地坐着，深陷
浓浓倦意。黑暗过道，
直到尽头，大门紧闭。
前方无猫眼^①眨着
绿光来迎接、蒙蔽
我们。当你将我们狠狠地
扔进不断收缩的幽暗
裂缝时，我投降，如腹中
眼盲、弯曲的婴儿，正在诞生。

① 猫眼（cat's eye）指安装于道路上，在黑暗中用来指示交通的反光道
钉。——译者注

Mercury

What tows it back tonight?
A bead of silver rolling among the stars,
and a jet's growl trailing behind its light.

One distant afternoon, the house in a drowse
between Hoovers and teatime, I creep in,
open his desk, slide out the drawers.

Caught from the broken barometer, harm
caged in a tobacco tin, humming, glamorous,
loose and luminous as a swarm.

The thought of it still shivers in the bone,
how it breaks into beads then shoals at the tilt of the tin.
Dangerous quicksilver. I'm alone,

while the grown-ups nap in their rooms.
Nothing to do but open things, touch the forbidden,
the whole, slow, summer afternoon.

It could get under your skin, electricity
running your veins, nerves, bones.

水银

今夜何物将它拽回？
一粒银珠翻滚在繁星之间，
而一架呼啸的喷气机则尾随其光。

一个久远的下午，房子在午餐
和茶歇之间酣睡，我悄然溜进，
展开他的书桌，滑出一层层抽屉。

毒物，从破碎的气压计里获得，
被囚禁在烟草锡罐中，蜂群般嗡嗡作响、
目眩神迷、悠悠忽忽，却光彩照人。

一想起它，我依旧毛骨悚然，不知
它如何破碎成珠而后涌入倾斜的烟草锡罐中。
流银，何其危险！我只身一人，

而大人们均在各自屋中歇息。
闲来无事，唯有东揭西启，触碰违禁之物，
以消遣那整个漫长的夏日午后时光。

它能渗透皮下肌肉之中，如同电流
游走在血管、神经和骨头之间。

It could light you up like a city.

A trick of the night sky and I'm there again, taking
a tiger out of a drawer, my promise, the law,
silence, his trust, my heart, all of it breaking.

它能将人如城市一般点亮。

一场夜空的小花招，而我故地重游，从
抽屉中取出一只猛虎时，我的诺言、那条法则、
那片沉寂、他的信任以及我的心都在土崩瓦解。

Welsh Gold

Two thousand years ago, before
he knew the word for *aurum*, *aur*,
a man was lured by a single yellow hair,
into the-gods-knew-where
of the underworld.
A sun-struck thread in rock,
filament of lightning, electric shock,
Apollo's pollens alchemised to gold.

A thousand years ago
in the scriptorium at Ystrad Fflur
a monk scribing its way across the page
a line of verse in Welsh from the Age
of Poets, heard a blackbird, clear
in the branches of an oak,
and dipping its feather in gold
touched an initial with a masterstroke.

威尔士黄金

两千年前，在人们
知道 aurum① 和 aur② 的对应词之前，
一人被一根黄色毛发所诱，
误入唯有神灵知晓
的阴曹地府。
岩中一条阳光垂照的丝线，
像极了闪电的细丝，一经电击，
阿波罗的花粉铸炼成金。

一千年前，
在花谷修道院的缮写室内，
一位修道士在纸上誊写了
一行源自诗人时代用威尔士语
写就的诗句时，听见了橡树枝头
一只乌鸫那清亮的啼鸣声，
他将其羽毛蘸了下金液，
精妙绝伦地点缀出姓名的一个首字母。

---

① 拉丁语中，指黄金。英语中，亦指黄金，不过该词已成为废词。——
译者注
② 威尔士语中，作为阳性名词指黄金，作为形容词指金色的。——译
者注

Here, in the mine, a trace
gleams on the worked rock face
like a line of verse on the wall,
a shaft of meaning, then illegible.
The gold has all but gone, its alchemy
undone like the illusion of money.

Sunlight on the river is fools' gold.
The real stuff's stored
in human muscle, blood and bone,
and an unrecoverable hoard
slips through our hands in the sea.

此处，矿井中，凿刻过的岩面上
留着微微发亮的一道道斫痕，
宛若墙上的一行行诗句，
那一道道深意，当时无法解析。
如今金矿早已消失殆尽，而炼金术
也随之泯没，犹如对金钱的幻灭。

洒满河面的阳光酷似"愚人之金"①。
真正的黄金储藏
在人的肌肉、血液和骨骼当中，
而难以复原的黄金宝藏
则从我们手中滑入汪洋大海之中。

① 英文原诗中 fools' gold，或许诗人化用 fool's gold 这一俗语，后指黄铁
矿，引申为看似黄金，实则一文不值之意。——译者注

Geographical Space and
Architecture

地理空间与建筑

St. Augustine's, Penarth

The church is like the prow
Of a smoky ship, moving
On the down channel currents
To open sea. A stone

Figurehead, the flowing light
Streams from it. From everywhere
You can see Top Church, remote
As high church is from chapel.

Church high on the summit
Of the climbing town
Where I was a child, where rain
Runs always slantingly

On streets like tilted chutes
Of grey sliding on all sides
From the church, to sea and dock,
To shopping streets and home.

Breasting the cloud, its stone

珀纳斯镇上的圣·奥古斯丁教堂

这座教堂犹如一艘烟雾
笼罩的船的船首，行驶
于溯游的航道上，
前往公海。其中一尊

石制的艏饰像，熠熠
生辉。这座山顶教堂
从四面八方皆可望见，却像
大小教堂之间那样遥远。

它高高耸立在
我儿时居住过的
小镇山头，那儿雨水
一律斜流，

将条条街道变成灰色
的斜槽，从教堂四周
滑落，流经商业街，
路过家门，直奔埠海。

高耸入云，它那

Profile of an ancient priest
Preaches continuity
In the face of turning tides.

古老神父的石像，
迎着翻腾的浪潮，
在布道永恒之光。

Lines

Diagonally the line
Dips between the trees
And the house. It wavers
Like the uncertain edge of a flag,
At the same time dividing
The space, charting one triangle
With clean white gestures,
And pegging together with small,
Desperate wooden teeth
The closed wound.

Ostensibly I lie
Sunbathing. I can feel
That wound of the divided
Mind: the upper triangle
Is rational. The aspens
Spinning leaves like florins
Up there in the light
Assert that it was good
For me, the pain.

线条

一条对角线
低垂在树林与屋舍
之间。它左摇右摆，
如同一面旗帜的未知边缘，
与此同时切分着
空间，以净白的姿势
勾描出一个三角形，
并用纤细的、
急需的木齿钉住
早已闭合的创口。

我看似躺着
沐浴阳光，实则能感受到
那种心灵裂开
的创伤：三角形的上部
神志清楚。一棵棵山杨
转动着枝叶似阳光下
旋转的弗罗林银币，
意在证明那疼痛
对我而言已是幸事。

Below

In the other part the blind
Blue, polythene pool,
Trawling coins and the dark
Sides of aspen moons,
Holds but sees no light.
The laundered people drown
In my pool. They wave
Their fistless arms, irregular
As images in a hall
Of mirrors.

At the end

Of the day I stood up, shook
The kaleidoscope,
Watching the circles and flakes
Of light falling, and a red
Plastic steamer going
Nowhere, bumping the sides
Like a moth at a shut
Window. The shapes fell
In a coloured muddle on the grass.
Neatly, slowly I folded
Clothes, and survived.

　　　　　而在
下部，一个令人目眩的、
蓝色的聚乙烯池子，
网罗了一枚枚硬币和一轮轮
山杨月亮的阴暗岁月，
容纳却不见光明。
浣濯之人曾溺死在
我的池子里。他们挥动着
无拳的胳膊，毫无规律，
恰如满厅的镜子中
所呈现的种种形象。

　　　　　长日
终逝，我便起身，摇动着
那个万花筒，
望着一个个光圈和光花
渐渐暗落，发现一艘红色的
塑料汽艇无处
可驶，却撞向两旁
犹如一只飞蛾扑向封闭的
窗户。各式形状，五彩斑斓，
拧成一团，坠落在草地上。
我缓缓叠好衣服，井然
有序，然后继续生活。

Clywedog

The people came out in pairs.
Old, most of them, holding their places
Close till the very last minute,
Even planting the beans as usual
That year, grown at last accustomed
To the pulse of the bulldozers.
High in those uphill gardens, scarlet
Beanflowers blazed hours after
The water rose in the throats of the farms.

Only the rooted things stayed:
The wasted hay, the drowned
Dog roses, the farms, their kitchens silted
With their own stones, hedges
And walls a thousand years old.
And the mountains, in a head-collar
Of flood, observe a desolation
They'd grown used to before the coming
Of the wall-makers. Language
Crumbles to wind and bird-call.

克利韦多格

人们结伴而出。
多数年老体衰，却恪尽
职守直至最后一刻，
甚至如常播撒豆子
那一年，终归渐渐习惯
于一台台推土机的脉搏。
高坡之上，座座园中，深红的
豆角花在水位涨至农场的颈部
数小时后才开始绽放。

唯有扎根之物幸存：
一片片遗弃的草料、一朵朵浸泡的
犬蔷薇、一座座农场、一间间堆满石头
而淤塞的厨房、一排排树篱，
以及一排排千古之墙。
而一座座山峰，被洪水的头项圈
锁住，注视着前方那片
筑墙匠到来之前它们早已
习惯的荒野。语言
崩塌，化作风啸与鸟啼。

Architect

E.A. Rickards (1872—1920)

Such a tonnage of Portland stone,
shipped to a coal town as the century turned.
Luminious, Jurassic, pure as stacked ice,
and marble from Sienna unloaded in the dirt
beside the black, black coal that paid for it.

Oh, to have been there, a hundred years ago,
Law Courts and City Hall complete,
flanking an avenue of sapling elms
among those sixty empty parkland acres,
there at the birth of a city;

to have stood that night with the young architect,
self-taught, flamboyant, garrulous,

建筑师

E. A. 里卡兹 [①]（1872—1920）

世纪之交，如此巨量的波特兰
石料被运往一座煤城。
侏罗纪时代的锡耶纳大理石，色泽明亮，
纯如冰堆，被卸在泥地里，
一旁则是用来以物易物的黝黑煤堆。

噢，似曾相识，一百年前，
在那开阔的六十英亩 [②] 绿地上，
有一条幼榆林荫大道，两旁
则是竣工的法院和市政厅大楼，
一座城市就此诞生；

遥想当夜，我陪同那位年轻的建筑师，
他无师自通，意气风发，口若悬河，

---

① E. A. 里卡兹（Edwin Alfred Rickards），1872 年 6 月生于伦敦，英王爱德华七世时期最杰出的设计师、绘图师、建筑师之一，擅长巴洛克风格的高层建筑设计，比如卡迪夫市政厅（Cardiff City Hall，1897 年）和威斯敏斯特卫理公会中央大厅（Methodist Central Hall, Westminster，1905 年）皆是其设计之作。1920 年 8 月 29 日于英格兰南部城市伯恩茅斯逝世，享年 48 岁。——译者注
② 1 英亩约等于 4046.86 平方米。——译者注

in love with high Edwardian Baroque;
to have shared his grand romantic gesture,
bringing a friend to view his work by moonlight,

to see his buildings carved from ice,
the clock tower's pinnacle, the clock
counting its first hours towards us,
when moonlight through long windows of the marble hall
cast pages yet to be written.

酷爱爱德华七世时期的巴洛克风格；
他那隆重的浪漫之风令我神往，
故携挚友月下共赏他的作品，

领略其各式各样的冰雕建筑，
还有钟楼的小尖顶，当挂钟
向我们敲响凌晨丑时的钟声时，
月光正透过大理石大厅的一扇扇长窗，
投射出一面面静待书写的篇章书页。

Senedd

Mountains spent time on it:
the slow settlement of silts,
mudstones metamorphosed to slate,
prehistory pressed in its pages.

Rock blown from the quarry face
and slabbed for a plinth, a floor,
a flight of stairs rising
straight from the sea.

The forest dreamed it:
parable or parabola.
Look up into the gills of fungi,
the throat of a lily.

A man imagined it:
the oak roof's geometry
fluid and ribbed as the tides
in their flux and flow.

He cools us with roof-pools of rain
that flicker with light twice reflected,

威尔士国民议会大楼

山体在它这里度过了悠悠岁月：
泥沙缓缓沉淀，
泥石硬化为板岩，
其书页记载着史前文明。

岩石从采石场的采掘面上被炸开，
被切割成石板，用作柱基和地板，
以及直接从海上
升起的悬梯。

森林梦见过它：
或是寓言，或是抛物线。
仰望它的菌褶，
好似一朵百合花的咽喉。

一人幻想过它：
那橡木楼顶呈现出的几何形状，
线条流畅，棱纹清晰，如同潮汐
起起伏伏，流动不止。

他设计楼顶上的雨池用来降温，
而雨池中摇曳着两次反射的光线，

a wind-tower of steel to swallow our words
and exchange them for airs off the Bay.

Inside the house of light at the sea's rim
you can still hear the forest breathe,
feel the mountain shift underfoot,
hear sands sift in the glass.

恍若一座钢铁风塔吞啮我们的话语，
然后将其置换成海湾吹来的空气。

身处这座光亮的海景房中，
您依旧能听见森林的吐纳，
能体会到脚下山体的移动，
能听到玻璃中沙子的筛响。

Taliesin

Frank Lloyd Wright 1867—1959

A house on a hill, Spring Green, Wisconsin.
From an outcrop of rock, an outcry of water,
he would curb the stone, harness the light of the sun,
bridle the great horse of the river,
raise walls, wings, walkways, terraces, a tower,
slabbed stone horizons on the shining brow.

The mark was on him before birth,
that single drop of gold his mother brought
across the Atlantic in the hold of her heart
from the old home in Ceredigion,
for her imagined boy, her child,

塔列辛 [①]

致敬弗兰克·劳埃德·赖特 [②]（1867—1959）

有一座房子坐落在威斯康星州春绿村的山头。
从嶙峋的岩石和咆哮的水流中，
他常常驯化石头，巧用阳光，
给河流这匹骏马套上缰绳，
筑墙、建配房、修人行道、搭露天平台、立塔楼，
在光亮的坡屋顶上铺设厚厚的石板层。

出生之前，印记早已烙在他的身上，
那是一滴金子，他的母亲
从锡尔迪金郡的故里携带而来，
用心捂着，横渡大西洋，
只为自己心中所设想的男娃，自己的孩子，

---

① 塔列辛（Taliesin）又译为塔里辛，被普遍认为是威尔士最早的诗人代表之一，此处是建筑名。——译者注
② 弗兰克·劳埃德·赖特（Frank Lloyd Wright），20世纪著名的美国建筑大师，生于1867年6月8日，具有威尔士血统，其母亲是一名教师，来自威尔士。他早期主要随父居住在艾奥瓦州（Iowa）罗得岛，求学期间立志成为一名建筑师。1911年，出版两部艺术著作，从此他在全球范围内声名鹊起。之后他定居在威斯康星州春绿村，并在该村的山上建造了自己理想中的家园和工作室，名为塔列辛。如今这处建筑成为美国威斯康星州一个著名的名人故居景点。——译者注

man of her making who would shape a world.

Raised in the old language, the old stories,
he learned his lines from the growth-rings of trees,
wind over water, sandbars, river-currents,
rhythms of rock beneath the ground he stood on,
colours of the earth, his favourite red
the rusting zinc of old Welsh barns, of *twlc* and *beudy*.

Taliesin, house of light, of space and vista,
corners for contemplation, halls for fiesta.
He sang a new architecture
from the old, in perfect metre.

twlc and *beudy*: pigsty and cow house

一位她所孕育的并将改变世界的男人。

他从小成长在古老的语言和故事中，
从树木的年轮、水上的微风、
沙洲、河流、脚下岩石的旋律
和大地的颜色中，
研习各种线条（诗行），而他酷爱的红色
则是威尔士那古老的谷仓、猪圈和牛棚①的锌锈色。

塔列辛，阳光之宅，宏阔之居，景秀之庐，
持冥想之屋隅，拥庆典之堂屋。
他以精妙绝伦的旋律，从旧物
之中吟造出崭新的建筑。

---

① 在英文原诗中，诗人用威尔士语 twlc 和 beudy 来指代"猪圈"和"牛棚"，并在诗歌末尾给出英文对应词 pigsty 和 cow house。——译者注

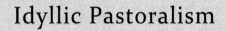
Idyllic Pastoralism

田园牧歌

Blaen Cwrt

You ask how it is. I will tell you.
There is no glass. The air spins in
The stone rectangle. We warm our hands
With apple wood. Some of the smoke
Rises against the ploughed, brown field
As a sign to our neighbours in the
Four folds of the valley that we are in.
Some of the smoke seeps through the stones
Into the barn where it curls like fern
On the walls. Holding a thick root
I press my bucket through the surface
Of the water, lift it brimming and skim
The leaves away. Our fingers curl on
Enamel mugs of tea, like ploughmen.
The stones clear in the rain
Giving their colours. It's not easy.
There are no brochure blues or boiled sweet
Reds. All is ochre and earth and cloud-green

布蓝科特 ①

你询问它的近况。听我娓娓道来。
它没有玻璃。空气旋转
于三角石架中。我们用苹果树枝
来温暖双手。丝丝烟气
升起,映衬着褐色的耕田,
向山谷四周邻里
宣告家中有人。
少许的烟气透过屋墙的石缝
渗到马厩之中,烟绕如墙上
的蕨苔。手里握着一条粗大的树根,
我将水桶下压穿过河
面,提起时,水流四溢,而后
移去落叶。我们的手指屈握
在珐琅茶杯上,像农夫一般。
雨中的石头,清新明亮,
焕发着光彩。它着实不易。
此处无小册子上所描绘的蓝天或甜美炙红
的景色,而是处处充满赭石、泥土和云绿色的、

---

① 布蓝科特是威尔士西部锡尔迪金郡下的一个农村破旧的农舍。吉莲在
二十世纪七十年代曾在这里住过。诗人以此作为诗题,反映了她的怀旧
情怀。诗歌追忆了威尔士山谷恬静的乡村生活,记录了远离现代化翠烟
袅袅的当地生活面貌,表达了对极简主义生活的向往。——译者注

Nettles tasting sour and the smells of moist
Earth and sheep's wool. The wattle and daub
Chimney hood has decayed away, slowly
Creeping to dust, chalking the slate
Floor with stories. It has all the first
Necessities for a high standard
Of civilised living: silence inside
A circle of sound, water and fire,
Light on uncountable miles of mountain
From a big, unpredictable sky,
Two rooms, waking and sleeping,
Two languages, two centuries of past
To ponder on, and the basic need
To work hard in order to survive.

味道酸酸的荨麻，空气里弥漫着润土
和羊毛的味道。那个由枝条和粗灰泥
制成的烟囱遮盖早已腐化，渐渐
化为尘土，如粉笔在板岩
地板上书写着各种故事。这里有着
高水准文明生活的基本
必需品：宁静
藏于声、水、火之中；
山川绵延万里，光芒四射，
天空浩瀚深邃；
两个房间，或醒，或睡；
两种语言，过往两个世纪，
等待思索；基本需求即
努力劳作，以便存活。

Birth

On the hottest, stillest day of the summer
A calf was born in a field
At Pant-y-Cetris; two buzzards
Measured the volume of the sky;
The hills brimmed with incoming
Night. In the long grass we could see
The cow, her sides heaving, a focus
Of restlessness in the complete calm,
Her calling at odds with silence.

The light flowed out leaving stars
And clarity. Hot and slippery, the scalding
Baby came, and the cow stood up, her cool
Flanks like white flowers in the dark.
We waited while the calf struggled
To stand, moved as though this
Were the first time. I could feel the soft sucking
Of the new-born, the tugging pleasure
Of bruised reordering, the signal
Of milk's incoming tide, and satisfaction
Fall like a clean sheet around us.

出生

某个极热、极静的夏日，
一头牛犊降生
在凯迪斯村野上；两只秃鹰
用翱翔来丈量天空的宽广；
夜幕渐渐降临，笼罩着
这一带的山头。只见蔓草丛生处
有一头奶牛，身躯肥厚，
静谧中透着阵阵的躁动，
沉默中发出异样的叫声。

晚霞消逝，星辰显现，
清澈明亮，一头滚烫的、湿滑的牛犊
终于降临，这时那头母牛起身站立，它那
冷却的侧腹似暗中的白花。
我们静静等待，只见那头小牛费力地
起身移动，仿佛这是它初次
行走。我隐约感受到了这头新生的牛犊
在温柔地吸吮，欢快地拉扯母牛
那青一块紫一块重新排序的腹胸。
不久，牛乳涌现，那满足感
似一床洁净的被褥裹在我们的身上。

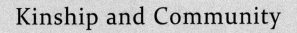

Kinship and Community

亲情与族群

Catrin

I can remember you, child,
As I stood in a hot, white
Room at the window watching
The people and cars taking
Turn at the traffic lights.
I can remember you, our first
Fierce confrontation, the tight
Red rope of love which we both
Fought over. It was a square
Environmental blank, disinfected
Of paintings or toys. I wrote
All over the walls with my
Words, coloured the clean squares
With the wild, tender circles
Of our struggle to become
Separate. We want, we shouted,
To be two, to be ourselves.

Neither won nor lost the struggle
In the glass tank clouded with feelings
Which changed us both. Still I am fighting
You off, as you stand there

凯特琳

孩子，我依然记得你的模样，
当时我在酷热的、白色的
屋里，站在窗旁，向外望着
红绿灯处
的人来车往。
孩子，我仍然记得你的神情，当时
我们之间发生了初次的激烈冲突，
你我在紧绷的爱的红绳上
拉锯争夺。那是一个苍白的环境，
四四方方，不受任何
图画、玩具的熏染。我的话语
写满了它的每一面墙，
你我那疯狂而又温柔的
相互挣脱渲染了
它那干净的方形空间。
我们渴望，我们呐喊，
一分为二，变成独立的自我。

我们曾经相互挣扎，不分输赢，
玻璃产房内，萦绕着情感，
改变着你我。如今我依旧
与你龃龉，你站在那里，

With your straight, strong, long
Brown hair and your rosy,
Defiant glare, bringing up
From the heart's pool that old rope,
Tightening about my life,
Trailing love and conflict,
As you ask may you skate
In the dark, for one more hour.

披着一头褐色的直发，又长又密，
你的脸色红润，
怒目中透着不甘示弱，这泛起
心池深处的旧绳
不断勒紧我的生活，
却印着爱和摩擦，
每当你问我你能否在漆黑中
再溜冰一个小时。

Community

We talk, especially at night
When we light fires and eat together.
I know my job, they know theirs.
We came here at random, drawn
By the place, related by love
Running like a fine metal
Chain through assorted beads
Forming between this and the next
A separate relationship.
One can stand aside and watch
The spatial movement, understanding
Edge forward, falter and change
Form. Or one can move in and feel space
Contract, aware of an approach.

I lay the plates on the table,
One before each, each one evidence
Of my concern for the man or child
Who pulls forward a chair and eats.
Our eyes sting in the smoky room.
We are tired early and take our turn
At the light of the fire to wash.

群居

我们叙谈，尤其在夜晚
一起生火、吃饭之时。
大家各安其位，各知其职。
我们不约而同来到此处，
被此地所吸引，因爱结缘，
犹如一条精美的金属
链条串联各式各样的珠子，
前珠与后珠相互连接，
却又相互独立。
或许你可以立于一旁，观看
空间的移动，领略
边缘的前进、蹒跚与变
形。抑或你可以进入，感受空间
的局促，警惕相互靠近。

我将碟盘放在桌上，
一人一个，无不证明
我对拉椅子吃饭的男士
或孩子的关爱。
屋内弥漫的烟雾刺痛着双眼，
我们早已倦意浓浓，轮流
在火光的照耀下洗漱。

I hang down my hair to brush it.
In the little house at night
We can hear each other breathe,
Turning in our beds, and things
Moving in the grass, and the leaves
Of the laburnum trees combing
The roof all night.

我梳着垂下的头发。
夜已深沉，小屋内，
我们能听见彼此的呼吸声、
床上翻身的响声、
草丛里的动静，还有
金链树叶那彻夜
梳刮屋顶的响动。

Swinging

At the end of the hot day it rains
Softly, stirring the smells from the raked
Soil. In her sundress and shorts she rocks
On the swing, watching the rain run down
Her brown arms, hands folded warm between
Small thighs, watching her white daps darken
And soak in the cut and sodden grass.

She used to fling her anguish into
My arms, staining my solitude with
Her salt and grimy griefs. Older now
She runs, her violence prevailing
Against silence and the avenue's
Complacency, I her hatred's object.

Her dress, the washed green of deck chairs, sun
Bleached and chalk-sea rinsed, colours the drops,
And her hair a flag, half and then full
Mast in the apple-trees, flies in the face
Of the rain. Raised now her hands grip tight
The iron rods, her legs thrusting the tide

摇荡

酷热的白昼结束时，细雨
飘至，空中激荡着耙过的泥土
气息。她身穿无袖连衣裙和短裤，
荡着秋千，望着雨水
从褐色的臂膀上流下，温暖的双手叠放
在纤细的大腿之间，注视着那些弹跳的白色雨珠变黑，
最后浸没在修剪过的湿草中。

她曾投入我的怀抱，常常向我倾诉
她的烦恼，而我的孤寂沾染了
她那盐苦阴霾般的忧愁。如今年龄增长，
她那随之而来的叛逆战胜了
沉默，撼动了那条林荫大道的
惬意，而我也变成了她的出气筒。

她的裙子，酷似躺椅那洗净的绿色，经受
阳光的漂白和白垩海浪的冲刷，将雨滴染上了色彩，
她的长发如同一面旗帜，在苹果树的桅杆上，
时而半升，时而全升，迎雨
飘扬。她那早已抬起的双手紧紧握住
铁杆，双腿将潮水般的雨水推向

Of rain aside until, parallel
With the sky, she triumphs and gently
Falls. A green kite. I wind in the string.

两旁，直到身体与天齐平，
她才洋洋得意，轻轻悠悠地
回落。一只绿纸鸢啊！而我卷绕着它的线。

Baby Sitting

I am sitting in the strange room listening
For the wrong baby. I don't love
This baby. She is sleeping a snuffly
Roseate, bubbling sleep; she is fair;
She is a perfectly acceptable child.
I am afraid of her. If she wakes
She will hate me. She will shout
Her hot, midnight rage, her nose
Will stream disgustingly and the perfume
Of her breath will fail to enchant me.

To her I will represent absolute
Abandonment. For her it will be worse
Than for the lover cold in lonely
Sheets; worse than for the woman who waits
A moment to collect her dignity
Beside the bleached bone in the terminal ward.
As she rises sobbing from the monstrous land
Stretching for milk-familiar comforting,
She will find me and between us two
It will not come. It will not come.

照看婴儿

我误入陌生的房间，照看着
陌生的婴儿。我不爱
这个孩子，尽管她酣睡时，
脸色红润如玫瑰，鼻孔冒着泡，皮肤白皙，
还算能让人完全接受的一个孩子。
然而，我害怕她。倘若她醒来，
她会厌恶我，会哭闹，
会在炎热的午夜里焦躁不安，她的鼻子
会流淌出恶心的鼻涕，还有她呼吸时
所带着香甜的芬芳难以令我痴迷忘返。

我无法给她任何的依靠。
对她而言，这将显得更加糟糕，
相比裹着单薄的床单心灰意冷
的恋人；不亚于在绝症病房内
漂白的骨头边稍等片刻
以重拾自己尊严的女人。
当她从恶境中呜咽着爬起，
伸手寻找那份乳汁般熟悉的慰藉时，
她会发现近旁的我，我们之间
并无隔阂。而它将不会到来！

Nightride

The road unwinding under our wheels
New in the headlamps like a roll of foil.
The rain is a recorder writing tunes
In telegraph wires, kerbs and cats' eyes,
Reflections and the lights of little towns.

He turns his head to look at me.
"Why are you quiet?" Shiny road rhythm,
Rain rhythm, beat of the windscreen wipers,
I push my knee against his in the warmth
And the car thrusts the dark and rain away.

The child sleeps, and I reflect, as I breathe
His brown hair, and watch the apple they gave him
Held in his hot hands, that a tree must ache
With the sweet weight of the round rosy fruit,
As I with Dylan's head, nodding on its stalk.

夜行

道路在我们的车轮下不断延伸，
在车头灯的照耀下崭新得像一卷锡箔。
雨仿若一台录音机，
在电报线、马路牙子、猫眼、
倒影以及小镇的灯光中谱写乐章。

他转头，望向我：
"为何沉默不语？"听着反光道路的节奏、
雨的旋律和挡风玻璃雨刷的唰唰声，
我用膝盖靠着他那温暖的膝盖，
而我们的汽车则将漆黑和雨珠甩开。

孩子已入睡，我呼吸着他那褐色的头发，
边思索边望着他那暖热的手里握着
他们给他的那个苹果，想到一棵树注定
因其圆润芬芳果实的重量而心痛不已，
我亦如此，因迪兰的头在它的颈上频频点头。

The Piano

The last bus sighs through the stops of the sleeping suburb
and he's home again with a click of keys, a step on the stairs.
I see him again, shut in the upstairs sitting-room
in that huge Oxfam overcoat, one hand shuffling
through the music, the other lifting the black wing.

My light's out in the room he was born in. In the hall
the clock clears its throat and counts twelve hours
into space. His scales rise, falter and fall back—
not easy to fly on one wing, even for him
with those two extra digits he was born with.

I should have known there'd be music as he flew, singing,
and the midwife cried out, "Magic fingers!" A small variation,
born with more, like obsessions. They soon fell,
tied like the cord, leaving a small scar fading
on each hand like a memory of flight.

钢琴

最后一趟公交车发出声声叹息，穿过熟睡的郊区车站，
再次伴着一连串钥匙的声响，他回到了家，走上楼梯。
我看到他又将自己锁在楼上的客厅里，
穿着那件巨大的乐施会① 大衣，一手悠然翻动着
乐章，另一手抬起那面黑翼。

在他出生的那间房里，我熄着灯。大厅里，
时钟清着它的嗓子，将十二小时数进
空荡的时空中。他的调时而高亢，时而踟蹰，时而低落——
单翼飞翔着实不易，尤其对于他，
因为他与生俱来地多了两根手指。

我当初本该知道他极具音乐才华，当他飞出时，大声歌唱，
助产士大声呼喊，"这双手不可思议！"与他人稍有不同，
天生多了几根手指，好像着了魔。不久，他们被切落，
捆扎得像脐带一般，留下小小的疤痕消退
在双手上，犹如飞逝的记忆。

---

① 乐施会（Oxfam）是一家致力于消除饥荒、贫困和不公的国际慈善机构，
总部位于英国牛津，由一群基督教新教贵格会（Quaker）成员、社会学家以
及牛津学者于 1942 年共同携手创立。"乐施会"的英文名字 Oxfam 是 Oxford
和 famine relief 的简写。——译者注

Midnight arpeggios, Bartók, Schubert. I remember,
kept in after school, the lonely sound of a piano lesson
through an open window between-times, sun on the lawn
and everyone gone, the piece played over and over
to the metronome of tennis. Sometimes in the small hours,

after two, the hour of his birth, I lose myself listening
to that little piece by Schubert, perfected in the darkness
of space where the stars are so bright they cast shadows,
and I wait for that waterfall of notes, as if
two hands were not enough.

午夜弹奏琶音、巴托克 ① 和舒伯特 ②。我依旧记得，
放学后，钢琴课上孤单的旋律时而响起，
透过敞开的窗户，而夕阳的光辉洒在草坪上，
大家都已离去，而他不断弹奏那首曲子，
伴随着网球的节拍。有时在短短的几小时之内，

在他出生的时间两点以后，我会陶醉在
那首舒伯特所谱写的小曲当中，享受此刻宇宙的幽暗，
当空耀眼的繁星投下片片阴影，
我在等待那瀑布般的流动乐符，仿佛
他那双手早已不够用。

---

① 巴托克全名是贝拉·维克托·亚诺什·巴托克（Béla Viktor János Bartók，
1881—1945），匈牙利作曲家，匈牙利现代音乐的领军人物，被认为是二十
世纪最伟大的作曲家之一。——译者注
② 舒伯特全名是弗朗茨·泽拉菲库斯·彼得·舒伯特（Franz Seraphicus Peter
Schubert，1797—1828），奥地利著名作曲家，被认为是古典主义音乐的最后
一位巨匠，同时也是早期浪漫主义音乐的代表人物。——译者注

Love and Friendship

爱情与友情

Dyddgu Replies to Dafydd

All year in open places, underneath
    the frescoed forest ceiling,
    we have made ceremony
    out of this seasonal love.

Dividing the leaf-shade as divers white
    in green pools we rose to dry
    islands of sudden sun. Then
    love seemed generosity.

Original sin I whitened from your
    mind, my colours influenced
    your flesh, as sun on the floor
    and warm furniture of a church.

So did our season bloom in mild weather,
    reflected gold like butter
    under chins, repeatedly
    unfolding to its clock of seed.

德诗谷答复达弗实

常年，在空旷之地，在
　　那壁画般的森林穹顶下，
　　我们应景相爱，
　　我们海誓山盟。

拨开遮蔽的叶幕，仿若潜水员
　　浮出绿池，斑白点点，我们起身
　　前往干燥骤照的阳光岛屿。不久，
　　我们恩爱得如胶似漆。

我将您脑海中的原罪
　　染白，我的颜色影响了
　　您的肉体，犹如阳光晒在教堂
　　的地面和温馨的器具上。

我们的爱情之花绽放在和煦的季节里，
　　折射出金色的光芒，如下颏
　　的黄油 ①，随着
　　花籽的时钟不断舒展开来。

―――――――

① gold like butter / under chins，诗人吉莲非常形象地描绘万物繁荣之季，
放眼望去，金光闪闪，如孩童采摘金凤花（buttercup）之后放在下巴，金
光闪烁，色如黄油（butter）。——译者注

Autumn, our forest room is growing cold.
  I wait, shivering, feeling a
  dropping sun, a coming dark,
  your heart changing the subject.

The season coughs as it falls, like a coal;
  the trees ache. The forest falls
  to ruin, a roofless minister
  where only two still worship.

Love still, like sun, a vestment, celebrates,
  its warmth about our shoulders.
  I dread the day when Dyddgu's once
  loved name becomes a common cloak.

Your touch is not so light. I grow heavy.
  I wait too long, grow anxious,
  note your changing gestures, fear
  desire's alteration.

The winter stars are flying and the owls
  sing. You are packing your songs
  in a sack, narrowing your
  words, as you stare at the road.

入秋时分，我们的林间寒意渐浓。
　我在等待，身体哆嗦，顿感
　日落西山，黑暗将临，
　而您的心正改变着这一切。

这个季节如一枚黑炭坠落，发出声声咳嗽；
　树木凄楚。森林枯萎，
　化为一片废墟，恍若一座无顶的寺庙，
　唯剩两人依旧在朝拜。

恩爱依旧，如一件阳光和煦般的圣衣
　披在我们的肩膀上，温暖又温馨。
　唯恐有朝一日，德诗谷，这个曾经
　备受爱慕的名字蜕变成一件素常的斗篷。

您的爱抚不再轻柔如故。我日渐忧郁。
　太久的等待令我焦虑不安，
　意识到您不断变化的姿态，担心
　日久变心。

冬季，繁星遨游，鸱枭
　吟唱。而您将自己的歌声塞进
　麻袋，变得沉默
　寡言，凝视着前方的道路。

The feet of young men beat, somewhere far off
   on the mountain. I would women
   had roads to tread in winter
   and other lovers waiting.

A raging rose all summer falls to snow,
   keeping its continuance in
   frozen soil. I must be patient
   for the breaking of the crust.

I must be patient that you will return
   when the wind whitens the tender
   underbelly of the March grass
   thick as pillows under the oaks.

Dyddgu is the woman to whom the medieval Welsh poet,
Dafydd ap Gwilym, addressed many of his love poems.

青年男子的脚步声响彻远山
　　某处。我殷切期盼女人
　　在寒冬有路可走，
　　有爱人在等待。

一朵怒放了整个夏天的玫瑰因雪凋零，
　　却在冻土中延长了
　　自己的生命。我应耐心
　　等待它的破土重生。

我也应静待您的归来，
　　届时微风吹白了三月草
　　那脆嫩的根部，
　　化作橡树下的厚枕。

作者注：德诗谷是中世纪威尔士诗人达弗实·阿普·格
维廉深爱之人，其诸多爱情诗便是为她而作。

161

At Ystrad Fflur

No way of flowers at this late season.
   Only a river blossoming on stone
   and the mountain ash in fruit.

All rivers are young in these wooded hills
   where the abbey watches and the young Teifi
   counts her rosary on stones.

I cross by a simple bridge constructed
   of three slim trees. Two lie across. The third
   is a broken balustrade.

The sun is warm after rain on the red
   pelt of the slope, fragmentary through trees
   like torches in the dark.

花谷修道院 [①]

深秋时节，花朵凋零。
　唯见河流，石上穿荡，
　漫山白蜡，硕果累累。

山叠林立，水流轻活，
　寺院守望，垡菲 [②] 青河，
　石上流淌，似诵宗经。

路过一桥，质朴窄小，
　三树所搭，两棵横卧，
　一棵残缺，竟作护栏。

雨后阳光，温润暖心，
　照耀红坡，树中散影，
　暗中摇曳，仿若火把。

[①] 花谷修道院（Ystrad Fflur）指威尔士锡尔迪金郡（Ceredigion）内一座十二世纪中叶建成、如今早已荒废的修道院，英文为 the abbey of Strata Florida。其中，Strata Florida 为拉丁文，Ystrad Fflur 为威尔士文，意为花谷。据说，此修道院曾是不少中世纪威尔士王公贵族的安息地，不少广为流传的传奇故事诞生于此，时至今日，此处依旧为不少威尔士文人雅士提供了创作灵感。——译者注

[②] 垡菲河（Teifi）是威尔士西南部锡尔迪金郡和卡马森郡（Carmarthenshire）的分界线，河流全长 121 千米。诗人在《族群之声》中指出英格兰文学与威尔士文学中一些意象有阴阳性的区别，比如英格兰文学中水通常是阴性，石头是阳性，而在威尔士文学中，正好相反。此首诗里的河流中有关于水、石以及周围谷地的描写，在河流译名上，译成中性之名更为合适，阴阳相济。——译者注

They have been here before me and have seen
   the sun's lunulae in the profound
   quietness of water.

The Teifi is in full flood and rich
   with metals: a torc in a brown pool
   gleaming for centuries.

I am spellbound in a place of spells. Cloud
   changes gold to stone as their circled bones
   dissolve in risen corn.

The river races for the south too full
   of summer rain for safety, spilt water
   whitening low-lying fields.

From oak and birchwoods through the turning trees
   where leaf and hour and century fall
   seasonally, desire runs

Like sparks in stubble through the memory
   of the place, and a yellow mustard field
   is a sheet of flame in the heart.

The medieval Welsh love poet, Dafydd ap Gwilym, was buried
at Ystrad Fflur.

万物栖此，胜我久远：
　　天上骄阳，水中弧影，
　　深邃宁静，祥和甜美。

垡菲河流，正值洪峰，
　　金属富饶，褐池之中，
　　金环闪耀，已存百世。

魔魅之地，我心着迷。
　　金云化石，恍如圆骨，
　　扬谷之中，消散流逝。

河水南流，夏雨充盈，
　　水流湍急，浪花四溅，
　　低洼之地，冲刷白净。

橡树桦林，或枯或荣，
　　叶落纷飞，时过世更，
　　季节轮换，欲望奔腾，

残茎星火，追忆此地，
　　原野芥菜，一片金黄，
　　恰似心火，熊熊燃烧。

作者注：中世纪威尔士爱情诗人达弗实葬于花谷修道院。

Love at Livebait

for Imtiaz and Simon

That time she stepped out of the rain
into the restaurant, and suddenly I knew.
Beautiful in her black coat,
her scarf that shocking pink
of fuchsia, geranium, wild campion,
and he at the table, his eyes her mirror.

She said she didn't know then—
but the light in her knew,
and the diners, the cutlery, the city,
the waiter filling our glasses with a soft
lloc-lloc and an updance of bubbles,
and the fish in their cradles of ice,
oceans in their eyes,

and all the colours of light in a single diamond
sliding down the window to merge with another.

爱情活饵

献给伊姆蒂亚兹和西蒙

那次，她冒着雨
走进餐厅时，我便心领神会。
她身穿一件黑色的大衣，披着
一条粉红色的围巾，惊奇地糅合着
灯笼海棠、天竺葵和野山葵的颜色；而他
坐在餐桌旁，双眸如镜，照出了她那楚楚动人的模样。

她说自己当时并不知情——
可她身上的光早已知晓，
当时的食客、餐具、这座城市也皆已知悉，
还有那位服务员为我们斟满酒杯时
所发出的轻柔"lloc-lloc"①声和不断升腾的气泡声，
还有那冰冷摇篮里的鱼儿，
和他们眼中的海洋世界，

以及一颗钻石融合了所有的光色，
从一扇窗滑落，与另一颗钻石合二为一。

----

① lloc 是威尔士语，意为折叠或钢笔，英文对应词是 fold 或 pen。此处诗
人主要将其作为拟音之用。——译者注

Later, saying goodnight in the street,
they turned together into the city and the rain.
On the pavement one fish scale winked,
like a moon lighting half the planet.

餐后，他们走向街头，互道晚安，
转身走进这座依旧阴雨笼罩的城市中。
在步行街上，一片鱼鳞扑闪着眼睛，
犹如一轮明月照耀着半个地球。

Still life

It was good tonight
To polish brass with you,
Our hands slighty gritty
With Brasso, as they would feel
If we'd been in the sea, salty.
It was as if we burnished
Our friendship, polished it
Until all the light-drowning
Tarnish of deceit
Were stroked away. Patterns
Of incredible honesty
Delicately grew, revealed
Quite openly to the pressure
Of the soft, torn rag.
We made a yellow-gold
Still-life out of clocks,
Candlesticks and kettles.
My sadness puzzled you.
I rubbed the full curve
Of an Indian goblet,
Feeling its illusory
Heat. It cooled beneath

平静的生活

今晚荣幸与您
一起擦亮铜器，
我们的双手略微沾着沙
和巴素擦铜水，好像
我们在海里待过，略带咸味。
仿佛我们将友谊
擦得锃亮，熠熠生辉，
直到欺诈或诡计
那所有被光所吞噬的暗锈
都被抹去。各形各色
不可思议的真诚
图案细腻地生长，坦然地
暴露在柔软破碎的抹布
压力之下。
我们从各式各样的钟表、
烛台和水壶中创造了
一份黄金般的平静生活。
我的忧伤困扰着您。
我抚摩着一个印度高脚杯
的完美弧线，
感受着它那虚渺
的温度。它在我的手指下

My fingers and I read
In the braille formality
Of pattern, in the leaf
And tendril and stylised tree,
That essentially each
Object remains cold,
Separate, only reflecting
The other's warmth.

渐渐冷却，而我从
图案的布莱叶盲文、
树叶、卷须
和风格独特的树中领悟到：
所有物体本质上
均保持着一份冰冷，
相互独立，仅仅反射出
对方的温暖而已。

Welsh Language

威 尔 士 语

Language Act

Eisteddfod 1993

We watch ourselves on television in the rain,
disputing our language in the other tongue.
The government messenger, come to view
the picturesque, is caught in the storm
under downpouring skies.

People we know, friends, acquaintances,
point at the ruddy Saxon face,
and have their say.
We lip-read his curses
bleeped from the soundtrack.

By now he'll be on the motorway,
or in the easing glow of the hotel,
towelling rain from his yellow hair,
shaking off the words like bees,
picking the stings from his skin.

We switch off the news, listen
to the rain falling fluent, filling

语言法案

1993 年威尔士民族艺术节

我们望着电视中的自己在雨中
用其他语言争辩着我们的母语。
一位政府信使，前来观看
如诗如画的场面，却困在暴雨中，
天空下着滂沱大雨。

故人、朋友、熟人，
一边指着红润的撒克逊脸，
一边发表自己的观点。
我们唇读着他从声道中
发出的刺耳魔咒。

此刻他估计在高速路上，
抑或在宾馆的柔光下，
拿着毛巾擦去黄发上的雨水，
抖落那些话语如同蜜蜂一般，
拔去肌肤上的刺。

我们关闭新闻，聆听
雨水畅流而下，充盈

the Bwdram, the Glowan and the Clettwr,

finding its tongue in the ancient dark

of the deepest aquifers.

布达郎、格洛湾、克勒特等地，
在那古老幽暗极深的地下蓄水层中，
寻觅自己的喉舌。

Translation

after translating from Welsh, particularly a novel by Kate Roberts

Your hand on her hand—you've never been
this close to a woman since your mother's beauty
at the school gate took your breath away,
since your held hot sticky hands with your best friend,
since you, schoolgirl guest in a miner's house,
two up, two down, too small for guest rooms
or guest beds, shared with two sisters,
giggling in the dark, hearts hot with boy-talk.

You spread the script. She hands you a fruit.
You break it, eat, know exactly how
to hold its velvet weight, to bite, to taste it
to the last gold shred. But you're lost for words,
can't think of the English for *eirin*—it's on the tip of your—
But the cat ate your tongue, licking peach juice
from your palm with its rough *langue de chat*,
tafod cath, the rasp of loss.

翻译

英译凯特·罗伯茨的威尔士语小说后有感而作

你的手在她的手上——你从未
与女人如此亲密过，自从在校门口
你母亲的芳容让你神魂颠倒，
自从你用又热又黏的双手拉着你的挚友，
自从你这位女学生住进了矿工的房子，
发现居住空间两上两下，作为客房或客床，
均显逼仄，与两位姊妹共居，
夜里咯咯大笑，畅聊男生话题，心潮澎湃。

你展开剧本，她则递来一粒水果。
你掰开它，吃了起来，心里清楚如何
握紧它那天鹅绒般的分量，如何咬，如何品尝，
直到最后一口福香。然而你早已顿口无言，
不知"eirin"[①] 的英文对应词——它就在嘴边——
猫却咬掉了你的舌头，用它
那粗糙的猫舌舔舐你掌中的桃汁，
猫之舌，失之铧。

[①] eirin 为威尔士语，英文对应词为 plums，指李树、李子、梅子。——译者注

Mother Tongue

You'd hardly call it a nest,
just a scrape in the stones,
but she's all of a dither
warning the wind and sky
with her desperate cries.

If we walk away
she'll come home quiet
to the warm brown pebble
with its cargo of blood and hunger,
where the future believes in itself,

and the beat of the sea
is the pulse of a blind
helmeted embryo afloat
in the twilight of the egg,
learning the language.

母语

你几乎无法称它为巢窝，
无非石上一道刮痕罢了，
而她战战栗栗，
绝望地发出呐喊，
告诫风与天。

倘若我们离去，
她便悄然归家，
回到暖和的棕色鹅卵石上，
那里覆满了血与饥，
那里充满了笃定的未来，

还有大海的拍击声，
犹若一个目盲的、戴着
头盔的胚胎的脉搏，而它悬浮
在蛋的曙暮光中，
正在学习语言。

First Words

The alphabet of a house—air,
breath, the creak of the stair.
Downstairs the grown-ups' hullabaloo,
or their hush as you fall asleep.

You're learning the language: the steel slab
of a syllable dropped at the docks; the two-beat word
of the Breaksea lightship; the golden sentence
of a train crossing the viaduct.

Later, at Fforest, all the words are new.
You are your grandmother's Cariad, not Darling.
Tide and current are *llanw, lli*.
The waves repeat their *ll-ll-ll* on sand.

Over the sea the starlings come in paragraphs.
She tells you a tale of a girl and a bird,

牙牙学语

这是一座房子的字母表——空气（air）、
呼吸（breath）以及楼梯的嘎吱声（creak）。
楼下（downstairs）响起大人们的喧闹声，
抑或当你入睡时他们发出的嘘声。

你正在学习语言：单音词
如坠落在码头上的"钢—坯"；双音词
如"布雷—克西"①的灯船；铿锵有力的句子
恰似一列驶过高架桥的火车。

后来，在弗雷斯特②，所学皆为新词。
你是你祖母的图图（cariad），而非宝贝（darling）。
潮汐和水流则叫浪潮（llanw）和流波（lli）。
波浪流经海滩时不断沙沙（ll-ll-ll）作响。

大海上空，欧椋鸟成片成群而来。
她向你述说一则女孩与鸟的故事，

---

① 此处应指布雷克西角，英文为 Breaksea Point，是威尔士南部海岸格拉
摩根谷（Vale of Glamorgan）吉尔斯顿林珀特湾（Gileston's Limpert Bay）
东部边缘的一个岬角，被称为威尔士大陆的最南端。——译者注
② 弗雷斯特（Fforest），地名，位于威尔士西部锡尔迪金郡（Ceredigion）
内。诗人曾在此短暂居住过。——译者注

reading it off the tide in lines of longhand
that scatter to bits on the shore.

The sea turns its pages, speaking in tongues.
The stories are yours, and you are the story.
And before you know it you'll know what comes
from air and breath and off the page is all

You'll want, like the sea's jewels in your hand,
and the soft mutations of sea washing on sand.

从散落在岸上那手写体般
的潮水中为你诵读。

大海翻阅自己的书页，说着各式各样的方言。
故事围绕着你，你却变成了故事。
在你觉察之前，你或许明白
空气、呼吸和书页所赋予的便是

你之所求，譬如你手中的沧海珍宝，
以及沙滩上那流动海浪的轻灵变幻。

Welsh

In the city I was born in,
it reached me like a rumour:
the name of a house, a suburb,
a word in my ear,
letters in family longhand.

It came down wires,
through walls in grown-up voices,
whispered behind hands,
pencilled in the margins
of Waldo and T.H. Parry-Williams.

The new lagoon has little to say,
safe from the surges of the Severn,
but at night, on the quiet, Taff and Ely
murmur at the harbour wall,
a sob in the throat of the sea.

威尔士语

在我诞生的城市，
它像流言蜚语一样向我袭来：
一座房屋和一个郊区的名字，
耳朵听到的词语，
还有手写的家书。

它顺着一根根电线，
以成人的声音穿透重重墙壁，
躲在捂着的双手后面窃窃私语，
用铅笔标记获胜者瓦尔多
和 T. H. 帕里 – 威廉姆斯[①] 的领先票数的差额。

新的潟湖无话可说，
免受那条汹涌的塞文河的侵扰，
但在夜晚，静谧时分，达夫河和俄丽河
对着港湾的墙壁轻声低语，
那是大海的喉咙在凝噎。

---

① T. H. 帕里 – 威廉姆斯（T. H. Parry–Williams，1887—1975），威尔士诗人、作家和学者。于 1912 年、1915 年分别在雷克瑟姆（Wrexham）和班戈（Bangor）赢得威尔士民族艺术节（Eisteddfod）的"王冠诗人"（颁给最佳自由体诗歌）和"诗座"（颁给最佳格律诗，是该国民文化节人气最旺的颁奖仪式）的荣誉称号。他是第一位同时获此两项殊荣的诗人。——译者注

And here in the square, the word's on the street.
Children chatter past my pavement table
as if they own the city, as if it's ordinary
to shake the dust off a rumour,
to shimmy and shout in Welsh in a Cardiff square.

广场上、街道上随处可见它的踪迹。
一群孩童叽叽喳喳，从我的户外餐桌旁走过，
俨然这座城市的主宰，仿佛将尘埃
从流言蜚语上摇落，并在卡迪夫广场上
用威尔士语起舞呐喊，皆不以为奇。

Patagonia

The year he didn't die,
he left on a banana boat
to convalesce at sea,
left me in teenage rage.

From his ocean-lit cabin, rocked
by the sleepless motion of waters,
he sent us deeps and shallows, shoals
and shinings in blue envelopes, the fin

of a whale breaking the surface where the nib
turned, his lines of longhand rolling
across fine pages, regular
as the sea's unfolding story.

Where are they now, those letters
like poetry of the sea?
I think she burnt them, feeding her need

巴塔哥尼亚 [①]

当年，他还在世，
乘坐一艘香蕉船
去海上康养了，
陷我于青春怒火之中。

他的船舱，在海洋的照明下，任由
海水夜以继日地摇晃，
他用一个个蓝色信封为我们寄来了
深海、浅海、浅滩和波光粼粼的味道，鲸鱼

那破海而出的鳍似转动
的笔尖，他那手写的诗行舞动
在精致的纸上，富有旋律，
宛若大海娓娓道来的故事。

那些信件，恰似大海的诗章，
他们如今何处？
我想她早已将它们焚毁，只为

[①] 巴塔哥尼亚（Patagonia）位于南美洲南部，包括阿根廷和智利的部分
地区。该地区以其广阔多样的地貌而闻名，包括山脉、冰川、峡湾和草原，
吸引了全球众多的游客和户外运动爱好者。此外，该地区有很大一部分
人说威尔士语。——译者注

to be free of it all.

Left, his voice on tape, found in his office
after the funeral, those interviews
from Patagonia in a strange Welsh,
his voice not like himself.

After sixty years I hear it better
in my head: "*Hwyl fawr*", he says to me,
last words, clear as a ship's bell,
before he turns to leave.

挣脱这一切。

唯剩他的录音带，葬礼之后
在其办公室里寻获，尽是些采访，
来自巴塔哥尼亚，操着奇怪的威尔士腔调，
听起来不像他的声音。

六十年后，我听得更加真切，
在脑海中：他对我说，"永别了"，
这句遗言，嘹亮得如海船的钟声，
之后他便转身离去。

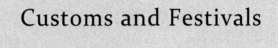

Customs and Festivals

风俗节日

St. Thomas's Day

It's the darkest morning of the year.
Day breaks in water runnels
In the yard; a flutter
Of light on a tiled roof;
The loosening of night's
Stonehold on tap and bolt.

Rain on my face wakes me
From recent sleep. I cross
The yard, shovel bumping
In the barrow, fingers
Stiff as hinges. Catrin
Brings bran and fresh hay.

A snort in the dark, a shove
For supremacy.
My hands are warmed
In the steam of his welcome.
Midwinter, only here
Do the fields still summer,
Thistlehead and flower
Powdered by hoof and tooth.

圣·托马斯日

这是一年里至暗的清晨时光。
黎明在庭院的小河沟中
迎来破晓；光线
在屋顶瓦片上翩翩起舞；
夜给阀门和插销上
的石箍咒正逐渐松解。

雨滴在脸颊上，将我
从新近的睡梦中唤醒。我穿梭
于庭院中，铁锹颠簸
在独轮车里，手指
僵硬似铰链。凯特琳
拿来麦麸和新鲜的草料。

黑暗里一声响鼻儿，一通乱挤，
力争上游。
我的双手在他
热情的迎接中变暖。
仲冬时节，唯有此处，
原野依旧夏意盎然，
虽则刺蓟和花朵
早已被蹄齿碾磨成粉。

Eisteddfod of the Black Chair

for Hedd Wyn, 1887—1917

Robert Graves met him once,
in the hills above Harlech,
the shepherd poet,
the awdl and the englyn in his blood
like the heft of the mountain
in the breeding of his flock.

In a letter from France, he writes
of poplars whispering, the sun going down
among the foliage like an angel of fire,

威尔士民族黑椅艺术节

缅怀赫德·温[①]（1887—1917）

罗伯特·格雷夫斯[②]曾与他相遇，
就在俯瞰哈勒奇镇的山上，
这位牧羊诗人，
血液中蕴藏着颂诗和警世短诗的基因，
犹如山峦的巍峨
在他羊群的繁衍中所占的分量。

在一封从法国邮来的信件中，他提到
白杨树窃窃偶语，太阳西落
在枝繁叶茂间，像一位赤焰天使，

---

① 1917 年威尔士民族艺术节的诗歌奖项颁发给了威尔士诗人赫德·温（Hedd Wyn），诗人却在艺术节举办前两个月逝世而未能亲临现场领取奖项。为了纪念他，威尔士民族艺术节委员会决定将其座椅用黑布罩着。此后，威尔士民族艺术节亦被称为威尔士民族黑椅艺术节（Eisteddfod of the Black Chair）。——译者注

② 罗伯特·格雷夫斯（Robert Graves，1895–1985），生于伦敦，20 世纪英国著名的诗人、小说家和诗评家，一生高产，著作题材丰富，代表作有自传《辞别一切过往》（*Good-Bye to All That*，1929）、历史小说《我，克劳迪亚斯》（*I, Claudius*，1934）、《诗选》（*Collected Poems*，1948）、诗论《牛津诗歌演讲集》（*Oxford Addresses on Poetry*，1962）等。——译者注

and flowers half hidden in leaves
growing in a spent shell.

"Beauty is stronger than war."
Yet he heard sorrow in the wind, foretold
blood in the rain reddening the fields
under the shadow of crows,
till he fell to his knees at Passchendaele,
grasping two fists-full of earth, a shell to the stomach
opening its scarlet blossom.

At the Eisteddfod they called his name three times,
his audience waiting to rise, thrilled,
to crown him, chair him,
to sing the hymn of peace,
not "the festival in tears and the poet in his grave",
a black sheet placed across the empty chair.

而朵朵花儿斜掩在枝叶中，
恍如孕育在一个废弃的壳里。

"相比战争，美愈加威武。"
然而，他听见了风中的哀伤，预见了
雨中的血腥，鲜血染红了片片原野，
而头顶上方乌鸦云集，
不久他在帕斯尚尔战役中跪倒在地，
双拳紧握着泥土，子弹击穿了他的腹部，
绽开出一朵绯红的鲜花。

艺术节上，观众三呼其名，
等着起立，满怀激情，
欲为他加冕、抬椅，
为他颂唱和平之歌，
而非"含泪庆祝坟中的这位诗人"，
将一块黑布盖在那把空椅上。

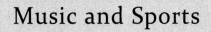

Music and Sports

音乐与体育

Singer

Something about its silence,
a black machine, gold finery lowered
and locked for good under the lid,
the stilled treadle, little drawers of silks,
spare needles rusting in their paper cases,

suggests a small foot rocking,
a delicate ankle bone in grey lisle
lifting and falling to an old heartbeat,
silk slipping under her hand
like the waters of the Glane beneath the bridge,

treadle and thread and woman singing
in another language sixty years ago
one warm June afternoon in Oradour,
before the sun fired the west window of the church,
before the last tram from Limoges.

歌手

它沉寂已久，
一台漆黑的机器，那金色的精致饰品低垂着，
永远地被锁在盖子的下方，
它的踏板原封不动，丝制抽屉小巧玲珑，
纸盒中躺着锈迹斑斑的备用针，

这无不暗示着纤纤细足曾在轻摆，
那柔美的踝骨裹在灰色莱尔线织成的长袜中，
随着悠久的心律此起彼伏，
丝线滑行在手的下方，
犹如桥下格拉讷河的水流，

脚踩着踏板，手摸着丝线，六十年前
一位妇人用另一种语言在吟唱，
那是在奥拉杜尔① 村一个暖洋洋的六月午后，
在阳光透过教堂的西窗射入之前，
在末班电车从利摩日② 启程之前。

---

① 奥拉杜尔（Oradour）即格拉讷河畔奥拉杜尔（Oradour-sur-Glane），
是法国中部利穆赞大区（Région Limousin）的一个村庄，曾于 1944 年 6 月
10 日遭受德军的大屠杀，全村 640 多条无辜的生命死于非命。——译者注
② 利摩日（Limoges）是法国中部利穆赞大区的首府，历史文化名城，被
称为法国陶瓷之都，素有"欧洲的景德镇"之美称。——译者注

The Accompanist

for Wynn Thomas

So the poem speaks
from the silence of the page,
father and daughter,
piano and voice,

Hard to say who leads, who follows—
poet, composer, singer or listener,
the reader or the page,
the voice or the piano

as she sings Fauré's "Lydia"
in a house by the sea
to the steadying sound of his hands
on the keys, the tide on the shore,

伴奏者

献给戚恩·托马斯

于是，这首诗
源自无声的书页，
恃凭父女的演绎，
随着琴声、歌声婉转悠扬。

无法辨明谁主，谁从——
诗人或作曲家，歌唱家或听众，
读者或书页，
歌声或琴声。

当她身处海景房内
吟唱福莱的《莉迪亚》① 时，
伴随着他那双手稳敲琴键
的声音，像极了岸上的潮起潮落，

---

① 《莉迪亚》（"Lydia"）是 19 世纪末和 20 世纪初法国著名作曲家和
管风琴演奏家加布里埃尔·福莱（Gabriel Fauré，1845–1924）创作的一首
有关爱情的音乐作品，其灵感源自 19 世纪末法国高蹈派诗人勒孔特·德·
利尔斯尔（Leconte de Lisle，1818–1894）的一首法语诗。该诗讲述了一
位象征着美丽与宁静的仙女般的神秘人物莉迪亚的故事。——译者注

and her voice becomes bird, takes flight
and she is Lydia haunting the evening
with something like grief, like joy,
and is more than music.

她的歌喉如同鸟儿，腾飞，
将她化身为莉迪亚，以似悲似喜
的心绪牵缠着这抹夜色，
而后飞离音乐的藩篱。

Bach at St. Davids

for Elin Manahan Thomas

In spring, fifteen centuries ago,
the age of saints, and stones, and holy wells,
a blackbird sang its oratorio
in the fan-vaulted canopy of the trees,
before Bach, before walls, before bells,
cantatas, choirs, cloisters, clerestories.
The audience holds its breath when the soprano,
like a bird in the forest long ago,
sings the great cathedral into being,
and apse to nave it calls back, echoing,
till orchestra and choir in harmony
break on the stones like the sea.
And listen! Out there, at the edge of spring,
among the trees, a blackbird answering.

圣·大卫教堂中的巴赫

献给伊琳·马纳汉·托马斯

十五个世纪前，某个春天，
那是圣人、圣石和圣井的时代，
在巴赫、城墙、钟声、大合唱、
唱诗班、修院回廊和天窗前，
一只乌鸫在树林的扇形拱状
天篷里演奏了自己的清唱剧。
而这位女高音俨然昔日林中的鸟儿，
用歌喉唤醒这座雄伟的教堂时，
在场的观众无不屏住呼吸，
歌声从半圆室到中殿频频回响，
直至管弦乐队和唱诗班和声协奏，
宛若海浪击石之声。
听！外面，树林之中，一只乌鸫
正应声附和，纵使春天姗姗来迟。

Advent Concert

Landâf Cathedral

First frost, November. World is steel,
a ghost of goose down feathering the air.
In the square, cars idle to their stalls, as cattle
remembering their place in the affair.
Headlamps bloom and die; a hullabaloo
dances on ice to the golden door.

Inside a choir of children sing, startled
at a rising hum over their shoulders
like a wind off the sea, boulders
rolled in the swell as, sweet and low,
Treorchy Male Voice Choir's basso profundo
whelms them in its flow and undertow,

and hearts hurt with the mystery,
the strange repeated story
of carol, candlelight and choir,
of something wild out there, white
bees of the Mabinogi at the window,
night swirling with a swarm of early snow.

降临节音乐会

蓝达夫大教堂

十一月迎来了初霜。世界坚硬如钢，
丝丝鹅绒弥散在空气之中。
广场上，一辆辆汽车悠闲地停放到位，恰似牛群
忆起自己应站之地。
一对对前灯此亮彼灭；一片人声鼎沸
飞舞在冰面上，迈向金色的大门。

门内，一群孩子齐唱颂歌，却惊诧地
听见身后传来一阵哼鸣，
似呼啸而过的海风，又似海浪中
翻涌的漂砾，而特雷奥奇男声合唱团中
一位男低音那温婉又深沉的音色
又将他们淹没在其乐曲的顺流与逆流中，

一颗颗心在赞歌、烛光与合唱中，
伴随那循环反复的神奇
故事而隐隐作痛，
而外面的世界略显狂野，窗外
飞舞着一群《马比诺吉昂》的白蜂，
夜随着纷飞的初雪旋转不息。

The Match

The legend goes like this:
The land is cold and bare,
when the people wake to a strange new hope,
and a mood of devil may care.
There is one with a silver boot,
and one with a raptor's stare,
and all of them young and strong with steel
and ready to do and dare.
There is one for the speed of the hound.
And one with a heart of a hare.
And millions to surge and urge them on to fly
on the wing of a prayer.
The cloud lifts from the land.
The sun stuns in the air.
When the ball goes straight through the golden gate
like a comet with streaming hair.
The bells will ring and people sing.
And we will all be there.

球赛 ①

神话如是说：
大地冰冷贫瘠，
人们醒来，面对陌生的新生希望，
如魔鬼心绪，若离若即。
此刻，一人穿着银色靴子，
一人带着猛龙般的眼光，
所有队员意气风发，健壮如钢，
蓄势待发，骁勇善战。
一人有着猎犬似的速度。
一人有着野兔般的心跳。
百万群众心潮澎湃，急盼他们翱翔，
戴着祈祷之翼。
云彩飘离大地，
烈日当空晕眩。
足球横穿金色球门
宛似一颗彗星，拖着飘逸长发。
钟声响起，人们齐唱。
我们终将凯旋。

---

① 该诗是诗人为2016年6月参加欧洲杯的威尔士足球队而写，歌颂
赞扬了球员的英勇，寄托了威尔士当地人的希望，并祝愿他们凯旋。
——译者注

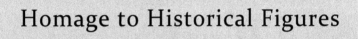

Homage to Historical Figures

怀古咏人

Hölderlin

for Paul Hoffmann

The river remembers,
then crumples in a frown of loss:
a garden of children and laundry at the brink,
the white face of a man shut in the mind's tall tower.

In the October garden, where the carpenter's children
played between the high wall and the water,
apples fall, and fire-tongues of cherry
crackle in the grass for us to shuffle.

The great willow that the poet knew,
only half itself since the hurricane,
kneels into a current that's deeper
and more powerful than it seems.

Upstairs, in his white, three-windowed hemisphere,
where for forty years they cared for him, light
shivers on the ceiling, bird-shadows touch and go,
things that were clear break up and flow away:

荷尔德林

献给保罗·霍夫曼

河流在追忆逝去的年华，
而后蹙起了失落的眉尖：
或是满园的儿童和堆放在园边的污衣脏服，
抑或是幽禁于心灵高塔中那张苍白的男性面孔。

十月的花园中，一位木匠的子女
嬉戏在高墙与溪流之间，
苹果从树上坠落，火舌般的樱桃
在草地上噼里啪啦，供人们曳步取乐。

这位诗人所熟悉的那棵大柳树，
飓风过境之后唯余半截，
跪倒在溪流里，而溪水
实则更深，也更激疾。

楼上，一个半球形的白色阁楼，带着三扇窗户，
他在那里被照顾了四十年，天花板上
灯光摇曳，鸟影若隐若现，
原本明晰之物如今七零八落、影影绰绰：

his poems on the wall,
quick freehand in the visitors' book,
a jar of flowers on bare boards,
a drift of red leaves on three windowsills.

So small, his bed must have been here,
his table there for the light, and the door
where the carpenter's daughter listened for his rages
and brought him bread, meat, a bowl of milk.

The swan turns on her own reflection. Silence
is her image. Currents pull. The willow
trawls its shadow, searching for something
in the broken face of water.

The river remembers everything, its long muscle
bearing the weight of rain a month ago,
the touch of waterbirds miles upstream,
the heavy step of a waterfall in its deep subconscious,

and the white, raging pages
that once beat their foreheads
on its scattering surface
before drowning.

墙上他那一首首的诗作、
来宾登记簿上所留下的速写笔迹、
裸露的木板上所摆放的那坛鲜花，
以及三扇窗台上所堆积的飘零红叶。

如此逼仄，他的床想必在这儿，
为了光亮，桌子想必在那儿，而门外
想必是这位木匠的女儿听他抱怨
并为他送上面包、肉和一碗牛奶的地方。

天鹅转身望着自己的倒影。默然
是她的形象。细水长流。那棵柳树
拽着自己的影子，在划破的水面上，
似乎在寻寻觅觅。

这条河流忆起了一切，用自身悠长的肌肉
承载着往昔一个月的降雨量，
拥抱着上游无数水鸟顺流而下数英里的触摸，
容纳着自身潜意识深处那道瀑布的沉重步伐，

还有那一张张咆哮的白页，
曾在淹没之前，
在涟漪的河面上，
猛拍它的前额。

Green Man

for Tony Conran

In your library I could have sworn I heard
the rustle of ferns rooting in deep crevasses,
the crackle of spores, a gasp of melting snow.
High-ledged among the spines of Yeats, R. S., Sorley,
the Mabinogi's streams, wilderness greened
in the stagnant water of jars.
Hart's Tongue. Lemon-scented. Maidenhair.

Later, that wet midsummer night—never mind
the rain—you made me climb your mountain garden,
a bit of pre-Cambrian tamed by the suburb.
The two of us tottered up, up in a stumble
through a drench of ferns and sweet mock orange,

绿人

致敬托尼·康兰 [①]

我确信在您的图书馆里我听见了
蕨类植物扎根裂缝深处时发出的簌簌声、
孢子嚛里啪啦的响声和白雪吁吁融化的喘声。
《马比诺吉昂》高耸于叶芝、R. S. 托马斯和索利
的书脊间，涓涓细流，而原野在坛坛罐罐
的死水中苍翠欲滴。
赤鹿之舌（山谷鸣）。柠檬香。铁线蕨。

不久，一个润泽的仲夏之夜——冒
着雨——您带我爬上您的山地花园，
一个供郊区居民开垦的前寒武纪的小山丘。
你我二人踉踉跄跄往上爬，
穿过重重湿漉漉的蕨类植物和娇滴滴的山梅花，

---

① 托尼·康兰（Tony Conran），当代英国盎格鲁-威尔士著名诗人、翻译家、剧作家、文论家。1931 年 4 月 7 日生于威尔士达费德郡（Dyfed）的蚌葛村（Bengal）。毕业于威尔士班戈大学英语和哲学专业，曾任教于母校班戈大学英语文学院。出版有《韵体诗》（*Formal Poems*, 1960）、《花神》（*Blodeuwedd*, 1988）、《城堡》（*Castles*, 1993）、《三场交响乐》（*Three Symphonies*, 2016）等诗集作品和《企鹅版威尔士诗歌集》（*The Penguin Book of Welsh Verse*, 1986、1992）等翻译作品。2013 年 1 月 14 日于班戈逝世，享年 81 岁。——译者注

and turned to see the glittering run of the Straits.
Polypody. Adder's Tongue. Brake.

I squint through a glass at the flipside of ferns—ovaries,
seed-sacs along each backbone like roe.
Like your poet's hands that stole the public road
for rhododendron and scented azalea,
spored with gold-dust as the pages of old books
for the making of poems, gardens, daughters.
Male fern. Lady Fern. Moonwort.

而后转身眺望那波光粼粼的海峡。
水龙骨。宽蛇之舌（犬齿赤莲）。凤尾蕨。

透过玻璃，我眯眼斜视着蕨类植物的背面——子囊，
即孢子囊，鱼卵般依附在每根脊骨上。
仿若您诗人的双手，为了杜鹃花
和香气扑鼻的映山红，抢占了公路，
并撒上了金粉，犹如一本本古籍的书页
用于作诗、建园和育才。
绵马（雄蕨）。蹄盖蕨（雌蕨）。月亮草（阴地蕨）。

The Poet's Ear

for Anne Stevenson

Nothing to do
with the clamorous city,
shouting sotto voce to no one
in pubs, parties, shops,
and all of us pretending to hear.

Nothing to do
with the train drumming the viaduct,
traffic tuning up at the junction,
the black stone cathedral's bells
in the frozen air.

诗人之耳

献给安妮·史蒂文森 [1]

与烦嚣的都市
无关，
酒吧里、派对上、商店中，
从不对谁温声细语，
而我们都在假装听着。

与高架桥上声响鼓振的火车、
十字路口蓄势重整待发的车辆、
凝固的寒气中
黑石大教堂敲响的钟声
无关。

---

[1] 安妮·史蒂文森（Anne Stevenson），1933 年 1 月 3 日生于英国剑桥，其父母为美国人，早期她因父亲任教耶鲁大学而随父定居在美国，1955 年嫁给一位英国人，随后随夫重回剑桥。她一生结过四次婚，丈夫均是英国人。1962 年以后，她主要定居在英国，曾在北威尔士短暂居住过。她年轻时在美国密歇根大学主修音乐专业，并获得学士和硕士学位，读书期间便开始诗歌创作。她曾出版多部诗集，比如《定居美国：诗选》（*Living in America: Poems*，1965）、《反转》（*Reversals*，1969）、《诗选：1955-1995》（*Collected Poems: 1955-1995*，1996）和《诗选：1955-2005》（*Poems: 1955-2005*，2005），还出版了一本有关西尔维娅·普拉斯（Sylvia Plath）的传记《苦涩的名声》（*Bitter Fame*，1989）。她晚年失聪，于 2020 年 9 月 14 日逝世，享年 87 岁。——译者注

Not wind in the feathering rusts
of the motorway angel
singing a note too high to hear,
its raps of red dust
in the slipstream of lorries.

Nor the small talk of ewe and lamb,
or the call of the kite and the crow
over Pwll-y-March
where high notes are first to go
in the labyrinth's silence.

It is footfall. Breath. The heart
listening for the line's perfect pitch.
It's not Bach, not Schumann,
but the mind's cello sounding
the depths of the page.

并非风披着高速公路天使
那羽状的斑斑锈迹
奏出高得离奇却难以闻见的乐章，
以及它在货车的滑流中
激起红尘的叩击声。

亦非母羊和小羊之间的轻声细语，
抑或风筝与乌鸦在普利玛赤小屋 [①]
上空发出的呐喊，
而是小屋那迷宫般的寂静中
最先响起的声声高音。

那是脚踏声。呼吸声。那是
聆听诗行完美音调的心跳声。
那并非巴赫，亦非舒曼，
而是心灵那把大提琴探寻
诗篇深处所发出的声响。

---

① 英文原诗为威尔士语 Pwll-y-March，是一座由石头砌成的小屋或小别墅
的名字，该石屋位于威尔士北部格温内思郡（Gwynedd）兰贝德村（Llanbedr）
附近雷诺格山（Rhinog Mountains）的山脚下，周围环境优美，视野开阔，
被广泛认为是一处极佳的旅游胜地。——译者注

The Fisherman

for Ted Hughes

From his pool of light in the crowded room, alone,
the poet reads to us. The sun slinks off
over darkening fields, and the moon is a stone
rolled and tumbled in the river's grief.

In a revolving stillness at the edge
of turbulent waters, the salmon hangs its ghost
in amber. On the shore of the white page
the fisherman waits. His line is cast.

The house is quiet. Under its thatch
it is used to listening. It's all ears
for the singing line out-reeled from his touch
till the word rises with its fin of fire.

The tremor in the voice betrays a hand
held tense above the surface of that river,
patient at the deep waters of the mind

渔夫

致敬泰德·休斯

在逼仄的屋里，诗人凭借一池的灯光
独自为我们读诗。在渐渐昏暗的原野上方，
夕阳悄悄溜走，而一轮明月恰似一块玉石
翻腾在忧伤的河流中。

在湍流的边缘处旋转着
一方宁静，鲑鱼将自身琥珀色的魂魄
悬挂其中。这位渔夫在书页般洁白的岸上
等待。他早已抛出了鱼线。

他的房子，一片寂静。茅草之下，
早已习惯了聆听。屋内，大家耸耳
凝听他从内心深处放出的吟唱鱼线，
直到言语带着激情似火的鱼鳍跃出。

微微颤抖的声音辜负了一只
在河面之上紧握的手，
它在心灵的深处耐心地等待，

for a haul of dangerous silver,

till electricity's earthed, and hand on heart
the line that arcs from air to shore is art.

为了能拽起一网危险的银色之物，

直至电流接地，手放于胸前，
而那条从天空到河岸的弧线则化为艺术。

A T-Mail to Keats

Dear John Keats,

I write to suggest that poets never die.
The old poetry drums in the living tongue,
phrase and image like bright stones in the stream
of common speech, its cadences a beat
that resonates as long as language lives.

I want to talk with you of the new nature,
of your grief at science for *unweaving the rainbow*.
But listen to the poetry of light,
the seven colours of coronas, glories, haloes,
how no two people see the same rainbow.

Oh, soon may science solve time's mystery!

一封遥致济慈的时空邮件

敬爱的约翰·济慈先生，

我写信旨在表达：诗人永不消亡。
古远的诗歌依旧鼓荡在现存的语言中，
词语和意象犹如日常用语这条溪流里
那些光亮的石子，只消语言尚存，
它的抑扬顿挫便会此鸣彼应。

我想与您聊聊自然的新气象，
还有您对科学"剖判彩虹"①的哀伤。
然而，敬请垂听光的诗情，
聆听日冕、荣耀和光环的七彩之音，
倾听缘何两人未能望见同一彩虹。

噢，唯愿科学尽早破解时间之谜！

---

① 诗人吉莲或许参考了英国学者理查德·道金斯（Richard Dawkins）
2000年出版的著作《剖判彩虹：科学、妄想与求知欲》（*Unweaving the
Rainbow: Science, Delusion and the Appetite for Wonder*）标题中的主标题
"剖判彩虹"。英文中将其首字母小写，其原因在于道金斯此书标题的
灵感亦源自约翰·济慈的《拉弥亚》（*Lamia*）一诗中有关彩虹的诗句
"So rainbow-sided, touch'd with miseries"（带着如此的彩虹色彩，多少有
点悲惨）。济慈在那首诗中探讨了科学与彩虹的关系。此处，诗人吉莲
就彩虹所展现出来的科学理性与诗歌感性之争做了回应。——译者注

Already words can take flight from our hands
over land and continents and seas,
with the small sigh of a shooting star.
If words can cross space, why not time?

In hope, I send this message into space.
May we meet over a verse, a glass
or two of the *blushful Hippocrene*,
a draught of vintage that hath been
cooled a long age in the deep-delved earth
in the ice-house of our refrigerator.

In esteem.
GC

伴随飞星的一声短叹，
文字早已能从我们的手中飞离，
越过陆地、大洲和海洋。
倘若文字能穿越空间，时间未尝不可？

我殷殷期望将此条信息发向太空。
愿你我能边会面边谈论诗词，雅饮
一两杯"鲜红的希波克伦灵泉"[①]、
一口贮存在我们冷藏库冰窖里
"那曾深埋于泥土中
冷冻良久的陈年佳酿"[②]。

此致
敬礼

晚辈吉莲·克拉克

[①] 为了致敬，诗人吉莲直接引用了济慈《夜莺颂》中第二节第六行的诗句 "Full of the true, the blushful Hippocrene"（充满真实的、鲜红的希波克伦灵泉）。Hippocrene 指灵感的源泉。——译者注

[②] 为了致敬，诗人吉莲直接引用了济慈《夜莺颂》中第二节开头两行的诗句 "O, for a draught of vintage! that hath been/ Cool'd a long age in the deep-delved earth"（噢！为了畅饮那曾深埋于泥土中/冷冻良久的陈年佳酿）。——译者注

Shearwaters on Enlli

for Michael Longley

Michael, the oldest known ringed bird
is a Manx shearwater, near sixty and going strong.
I choose it as *llatai*, bird-messenger, sea-crier
for the poet of flight and song.

Midnight, midsummer, and almost dark
but for the loom of Dublin at the rim of the world,
flocks of shearwaters home in from the sea,
like the souls of twenty thousand saints
come to reclaim their holy remains.

They flare in the sweep of the lighthouse beam,
a sigh of sparks, an outcry of angels, a scream
as if they feel it, the shock of the light
then the dark after the long day's flight
in the troughs of the waves.

Doused one by one, each footless bird to its burrow.

恩利岛① 上的剪水鹱

献给迈克尔·朗利

迈克尔，世上已知最为古老的环斑鸟
是一只源自马恩岛的剪水鹱，年近六旬，依旧强健。
我将它选为"飒泰"，一种信鸟，海上信使，
赠予这位不断翱翔与吟唱的诗人。

盛夏的午夜，除了地平线上隐约
见到都柏林的掠影外，黑暗几乎笼罩了一切，
而剪水鹱成群结队地从海上归家，
犹如两万名圣者的灵魂
前来索回自己的圣骸。

在灯塔环射的光束中，它们熠熠生辉，
发出星火般的叹息和天使般的呐喊与惊鸣，
似乎它们早已感知：在海浪的波谷中，
经历白天漫长的飞翔后，
那明暗交替所带来的震撼。

这些无足的鸟儿，陆续被吹熄，返回自己的巢穴。

① Enlli 是威尔士语，即 Ynys Enlli，英语是 Bardsey Island，即巴德西岛。
——译者注

241

And I to mine, a damp nest in the lighthouse,
every swing of the beam a wing feathered with gold
fires the room all night, a blaze against the cold.

Enlli: Bardsey Island

而我也回到家中，一个似灯塔里湿漉漉的巢穴，
光束每次的摇摆便让每对羽翼披上了金色
烈焰彻夜烘明这间塔房，御寒防冷。

作者注：恩利岛即巴德西岛。

The Plumber

Harry Patch 1898—2009

He'd often work crouched on the floor
his toolbag agape beside him
like a wound.

He'd choose spanner or wrench,
tap for an airlock, blockage, leak,
for water's sound.

Not a man for talk. His work
a translation, his a clean trade
for silent hands.

Sweet water washed away waste,

水暖工

致敬哈里·帕奇 ^①（1898—2009）

他常蜷伏在地板上工作，
而身旁的工具包敞开着，
犹如一道伤口。

他常会用扳手或扳钳，
轻轻敲打，检查气塞、堵塞、漏水，
听听水声。

他不善言谈。他的工作
恰似翻译，一种干净的交易
为了沉默的双手。

甘泉涤荡了一切的氛秽，

------

① 哈里·帕奇（Harry Patch），英国最后一名一战老兵，1898 年 6 月 17 日
生于英格兰萨默塞特郡（Somerset）。1914 年加入康沃尔公爵轻步兵团（the
Duke of Cornwall's Light Infantry）。1915 年、1917 年参加了法国的索姆河战
役（the Battle of the Somme）和帕申戴尔战役（the Battle of Passchendaele），
在两次战役中均受了伤，之后回国，于 1918 年退伍。一战后，做过石匠和
水管工，同时因对一切的战争直言不讳，积极倡导和平运动，反对一切形
式的暴力而闻名。2009 年 7 月 25 日逝世，享年 111 岁。——译者注

the mud, the blood, the dirt,
the dead, the drowned,

the outcry, outfall, outrage of war
transformed
to holy ground.

如战中的泥浆、鲜血、
污尘、死者、溺者、

呐喊、冲锋和愤怒，
将其变为
一片圣土。

The Book of Aneirin

Sorrow sharp as yesterday, a lament
passed down and learned by heart
until that moment
when the scribe began to write.

Fifteen centuries later,
words still hymn their worth,
young men, all but one slaughtered,
lost in the hills of the Old North.

Blood-ballad
of the battlefield,
on quires of quiet pages, laid leaf
on leaf like strata of stone, Aneirin's grief.

The Book of Aneirin: the thirteenth-century manuscript of a
sixth-century poet

阿尼林之书 ①

悲伤猛烈如昔，若一首挽歌
众口相传，熟记于心，
直到一位文士
开始将它记录下来。

十五个世纪之后，
所载文字依旧焕发着光辉，
所有青年，除一人幸存之外，皆遭屠杀，
湮灭在古远北方的冈峦之中。

战场上
那泣血的歌谣，
躺在一摞阒寂的纸上，页页
相叠俨如石层，述说着阿尼林之哀。

作者注：《阿尼林之书》是一部关于六世纪诗人阿尼林
的诗歌手稿，成书于十三世纪。

---

① 阿尼林（Aneirin）又译为阿尼瑞，公元 6 世纪威尔士诗人，其代表作
《高多汀部落的哀歌》（"Y Gododdin"）被认为是现存威尔士最古老的
诗歌作品之一，收录在《阿尼林之书》（*The Book of Aneirin*）中，馆藏
于卡迪夫城市图书馆。——译者注

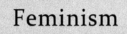

Feminism

女性主义

Death of a Young Woman

She died on a hot day. In a way
Nothing was different. The stretched white
Sheet of her skin tightened no further.
She was fragile as a yacht before,
Floating so still on the blue day's length,
That one would not know when the breath
Blew out and the sail finally slackened.
Her eyes had looked opaquely in the
Wrong place to find those who smiled
From the bedside, and for a long time
Our conversations were silent.

The difference was that in her house
The people were broken by her loss.
He wept for her and for the hard tasks
He had lovingly done, for the short,
Fierce life she had lived in the white bed,
For the burden he had put down for good.
As we sat huddled in pubs supporting
Him with beer and words' warm breath,
We felt the hollowness of his release.

少妇之死

她死于酷热之日。仿佛
一切照旧。她那洁白如纸的肌肤
舒展开后便不复紧致之感。
生前她虚弱得像一艘帆船，
静谧地悬浮在碧蓝的天地之间，
无人知晓她的呼吸何时
停息，风帆何时松垂。
当床前有人微笑地探望时，
她的双眸早已无光，显得呆滞，
常常望向别处，而我们沉默
良久，互无交流。

生者有别：在逝者家中，
人们因其离去而悲痛不已。
他为她伤心落泪，为自己曾心甘情愿
的辛苦付出而哽咽，他忧伤她
在白色的床榻上度过了短暂而艰辛的人生，
哀叹自己如今终于卸下了重担。
当我们挤坐在酒吧里，陪伴他，
与他共饮，并用暖语抚慰他的心灵时，
发现他的如释重负中却带着几分空虚。

Our own ungrateful health prowled, young,
Gauche about her death. He was polite,
Isolated. Free. No point in going home.

年轻的我们带着负德孤恩的健康踯躅着，
对她的离世显得幼稚粗俗。而谦谦有礼的他
形影相吊。虽已解脱，归家却毫无意义。

Letter from a Far Country

They have gone. The silence resettles
slowly as dust on the sunlit
surfaces of the furniture.
At first the skull itself makes
sounds in any fresh silence,
a big sea running in a shell.
I can hear my blood rise and fall.

Dear husbands, fathers, forefathers,
this is my apologia, my
letter home from the future,
my bottle in the sea which might
takes a generation to arrive.

The morning's all activity.
I draw the detritus of a family's
loud life before me, a snow plough,
a road-sweeper with my cart of leaves.
The washing machine drones
in the distance. From time to time
as it falls silent I fill baskets
with damp clothes and carry them

远乡来信

他们已走。宁静缓缓
重新落定，犹如阳光照射下，
家具表面上的尘埃。
起初头颅自身发出
声音，响彻在每一片宁静中，
大海在贝壳中奔流。
我仿佛听到了自己的血液此起彼伏。

亲爱的丈夫们、父亲们、祖先们，
这是我的道歉，一封
从未来寄回的家书，
我那海中的漂流瓶兴许
要耗费一代人的时光方能抵达。

早上全是忙活。
我来描绘下眼前一个家庭
喧嚣琐碎的生活：一把雪梨，
一台扫路车拉着一车的树叶。
远处洗衣机嗡嗡
作响。经常
当它停下不响时，我将微湿的衣服
放进筐中，之后提到

into the garden, hang them out,
stand back, take pleasure counting
and listing what I have done.
The furniture is brisk with polish.
On the shelves in all of the rooms
I arrange the books
in alphabetical order
according to subject: Mozart,
Advanced Calculus, William
and Paddington Bear.
Into the drawers I place your clean
clothes, pyjamas with buttons
sewn back on, shirts stacked neatly
under their labels on the shelves.

The chests and cupboards are full,
the house sweet as a honeycomb.
I move in and out of the hive
all day, harvesting, ordering.
You will find all in its proper place,
when I have gone.

As I write I am far away.
First see a landscape. Hill country,
essentially feminine,
the sea not far off. Its blues

花园去，将衣服挂起后，
往后一站，开心地细数、
罗列自己所做之事。
家具擦得油光发亮。
所有屋内的书架上，
我将书籍
按字母顺序摆放，
按主题分类：莫扎特、
高等微积分、威廉
和帕丁顿熊。
我将你那干净的衣服放入
抽屉，重新给睡衣
缝上纽扣，叠好衬衣，
按标签放在架子上，并然有序。

箱子、橱柜满满登登，
房屋香甜如蜂巢。
我整日进进出出
这个巢，不停收获和整理。
当我不在时，
你们会发现他们皆各安其位。

提笔写信时，我已身在远方。
首先领略风景。山村，
核心是女性化，
不远处可见大海。海之蓝

widen the sky. Bryn Isaf
down there in the crook of the hill
under Calfaria's single eye.
My grandmother might have lived there.
Any farm. Any chapel.
Father and minister, on guard,
close the white gates to hold her.

A stony track turns between
ancient hedges, narrowing,
like a lane in a child's book.
Its perspective makes the heart restless
like the boy in the rhyme, his stick
and cotton bundle on his shoulder.

The minstrel boy to the war has gone.
But the girl stays. To mind things.
She must keep. And wait. And pass time.

There's always been time on our hands.
We read this perfectly white page
for the black head of the seal,
for the cormorant, as suddenly gone
as a question from the mind,

延展碧空之阔。下方一间山谷农舍
坐落在山间溪流之中，
位于卡尔法力亚教堂^①的单眼下方。
我的祖母或许就生活在那里。
每一座农场。每一座小教堂。
神父和牧师，站哨执勤，
紧闭白色大门，守护着她。

古老篱笆间蜿蜒着
一条石路，渐渐变窄，
像儿童读物里的小巷。
它的视角令人心旌摇曳，
像踏着旋律的男孩，肩上扛着
一根棍棒和一捆棉花。

这位吟游男孩早已参战去了。
而这位女孩却选择留下，料理家务。
她必须坚守，等待，消磨时光。

我们总有闲暇时光。
我们读着这洁白无瑕的一页，
为了能一睹海豹的乌黑脑袋
和鸬鹚的芳容，生怕突然消失，
恰似脑海中闪现的问题，

---

① 卡尔法力亚教堂位于南威尔士阿伯代尔城镇，是该城镇所在山谷地区
中最大的浸信会教堂之一。——译者注

snaking underneath the surfaces.
A cross of gull shadow on the sea
as if someone stepped on its grave.
After an immeasurable space
the cormorant breaks the surface
as a small, black, returning doubt.

From here the valley is narrow,
the lane lodged like a halfway ledge.
From the opposite wood the birds
ring like a tambourine. It's not
the birdsong of a garden, thrush
and blackbird, robin and finch,
distinguishable, taking turn.
The song's lost in saps and seepings,
amplified by hollow trees,
cupped leaves and wind in the branches.
All their old conversations
collected carefully, faded
and difficult to read, yet held
forever as voices in a well.

Reflections and fallen stones; shouts
into the scared dark of lead-mines;
the ruined warehouse where the owls stare;
sea-caves; cellars; the back stairs

迂回前进于水下。
海鸥掠影于海上
犹如人踩在墓地上。
游了一段深不可测的水域后，
那只鸬鹚破水而出，
仿若一个折返的疑问，又小又黑。

从此处眺望，山谷狭小，
道路嵌入得像半截的岩架。
鸟儿在对面的树林里
小手鼓般低吟。不像
园中画眉鸟、燕八哥、
知更鸟、燕雀的轮流
鸣叫那样清晰可辨。
歌声消退在树液和渗浆中，
音量被中空的树木、
翘曲的叶子、枝干里的风增强放大。
他们间所有古老的对话
被细心地收集着，褪色，
难以卒读，却被永远地
保存，似井中之声。

倒影、坠石；呐喊
朝向铅矿那恐怖的幽暗处；
废弃的仓库里猫头鹰凝视着；
海洞、地窖、雪尼尔花线

behind the chenille curtain;
the landing when the lights are out;
nightmares in hot feather beds;
the barn where I'm sent to fetch Taid;
that place where the Mellte flows
boldly into limestone caves
and leaps from its hole a mile on,
the nightmare still wild in its voice.

When I was a child a young boy
was drawn into a pipe and drowned
at the swimming pool. I never
forgot him, and pity rivers
inside mountains, and the children
of Hamelin sucked in by music.
You can hear children crying
from the empty woods.
It's all given back in concert
with the birds and leaves and water
and the song and dance of the Piper.

Listen! To the starlings glistening
on a March morning! Just one day
after snow, an hour after frost,
the thickening grass begins to shine
already in the opening light.

窗帘后面的侧面楼梯；
梯台处熄灭的灯光；
梦魇生于滚热的羽毛床上；
在谷仓我被叫去接祖母；
梅尔特河途经那儿，
勇猛地流进石灰岩洞中，
在洞口跃起一米高，
噩梦仍旧疯狂呼啸。

在我小的时候，一位年轻小伙子
被吸入管道中，之后溺死
在泳池中。我从未
忘记他，可惜山中
的河流、哈梅林
的孩童们被音乐吞噬。
你会听到孩童的哭泣
响彻整片空林。
一切仿佛像音乐会一般
与鸟儿、树叶、水、
吹笛者的歌舞完美地融合。

听！欧椋鸟在三月
清晨闪动！雪后
有一日，霜后一小时，
肥厚的草地开始
在天光初开中发亮。

There's wind to rustle the blood,
the sudden flame of crocus.

My grandmother might be standing
in the great silence before the Wars.
Hanging the washing between trees
over the white and the red hens.
Sheets, threadworked pillowcases.
Mamgu's best pais, her Sunday frock.

The sea stirs restlessly between
the sweetness of clean sheets,
the lifted arms,
the rustling petticoats.

My mother's laundry list, ready
on Mondays when the van called.
The rest soaked in glutinous starch
and whitened with a bluebag
kept in a broken cup.

(In the airing cupboard you'll see
a map, numbering and placing
every towel, every sheet.
I have charted all your needs.)

风吹着如血如火焰般
的番红花飒飒作响。

我的祖母可能正身处
战前那段巨大的沉寂中：
在一群红白母鸡的上方，
她将洗好的衣物晾在树间。
有床单、线纺的枕头。
还有祖母最好的外衣、周日穿的连衣裙。

大海无休止地翻动
在清香洁净的床单、
举起的臀部
和沙沙作响的衬裙之间。

我母亲的洗衣清单，已备好，
每当周一货车被叫来时。
剩下的浸在黏稠的米浆中，
随着漏杯中的蓝袋漂白剂
一起漂白。

（晾衣橱内你会发现
一张地图，标记并摆放了
每一条毛巾、每一条床单。
我已记下你所需之物。）

It has always been a matter
of lists. We have been counting,
folding, measuring, making,
tenderly laundering cloth
ever since we have been women.

The waves are folded meticulously,
perfectly white. Then they are tumbled
and must come to be folded again.

Four herring gulls and their shadows
are shouting at the clear glass
of a shaken wave. The sea's a sheet
bellying in the wind, snapping.
Air and white linen. Our airing cupboards
are full of our satisfactions.

The gulls grieve at our contentment.
It is a masculine question.
"Where" they call "are your great works?"
They slip their fetters and fly up
to laugh at land-locked women.
Their cries are cruel as greedy babies.

Our milky tenderness dry
to crisp lists; immaculate

一直都在
罗列清单。我们忙于计算、
折叠、测量、制作，
以及轻洗布料，
自从我们成为女人以来。

波浪似的床单被小心翼翼地折叠好，
无比白净。然后他们被翻滚，
须再度被折叠好。

四只鲭鸥及他们的倩影
朝着玻璃般清澈的、
摇动的波浪呐喊。大海如床单
在风中鼓胀，突然崩裂。
空气和白色亚麻布。我们的烘柜
洋溢着我们的遂心如意。

鲭鸥哀怨我们的知足。
这是一个男性的问题。
"您的杰作"他们喊着"如今何在？"
他们摆脱束缚，振翼起飞
来嘲笑陆封的女人。
他们冷酷的哭喊如同贪婪的婴儿。

我们乳白色的稚嫩日渐干枯，
献给各种日常清单；床单被罩

linen; jars labelled and glossy
with our perfect preserves.
Spiced oranges; green tomato
chutney; Seville orange marmalade
annually staining gold
the snows of January

(the saucers of marmalade
are set when the amber wrinkles
like the sea if you blow it)

Jams and jellies of blackberry,
crabapple, strawberry, plum,
greengage and loganberry.
You can see the fruit pressing
their little faces against the glass;
tiny onions imprisoned
in their preservative juices.

Familiar days are stored whole
in bottles. There's a wet morning
orchard in the dandelion wine;
a white spring distilled
in elderflower's clarity;
and a loving, late, sunburning
day of October in syrups

洁白无瑕；罐子贴好标签，色泽光亮
均被我们完美保存。
五香橘子、绿色番茄
酸辣酱、塞维利亚橘子酱
将每年一月的飘雪
染成了金黄。

（将盛果酱的碟子
——摆好，而琥珀起皱得
像大海一般，倘若你向它吹气。）

各种果酱和果冻：黑莓、
红果、草莓、李子、
青梅和罗甘莓。
你会看到水果将
小脸蛋贴在玻璃上；
细小的洋葱被囚禁
在他们的腌汁里。

熟悉的光阴被完整地储存
在瓶瓶罐罐中。蒲公英美酒里
藏着一座湿润的清晨果园；
白色泉水蒸馏
在清澈的接骨木花酒中；
一个爱意浓浓、晚至、炎热的
十月秋日藏在野玫瑰

of rose hip and the beautiful
black sloes that stained the gin to rose.

It is easy to make of love
these ceremonials. As priests
we fold cloth, break bread, share wine,
hope there's enough to go round.

(You'll find my inventories pinned
inside all of the cupboard doors.)

Soon they'll be planting the barley.
I imagine I see it, stirring
like blown sand, feel the stubble
cutting my legs above blancoed
daps in a summer too hot
for Wellingtons. The cans of tea
swing squeakily on wire loops,
outheld, not to scald myself,
over the ten slow leagues
of the field of golden knives.
To be out with the men, at work,
I had longed to carry their tea,

果糖浆剂中，而美丽的
黑色野李将杜松子酒染成了玫瑰色。

在这些仪式中能随处
感受到爱。作为祭司，
我们叠布、掰面包、分酒，
希望足够绕桌分配。

（你会发现我的存货钉
在所有橱柜的门内。）

不久，他们将要种植大麦。
我设想看到了此景，心潮澎湃
如吹起的沙子，感到麦茬
割着我的双腿，脚上穿着布兰可
擦白剂擦过的橡皮底帆布鞋，夏天
穿威灵顿长筒靴太热。各种茶罐
吱吱呀呀地摇晃在铁线环上，
我往外提着，生怕烫伤自己，
行走在那漫长广阔的 [①]
金刀麦地上。
和男人外出干活儿，
我一直想着帮他们提茶，

---

① 英文原诗是 ten slow leagues。league 即里格，欧洲和拉丁美洲一个古老
的长度单位，1 里格约等于 4.828 千米，相当于步行一小时的距离。此处
是虚词，形容麦地非常宽广。——译者注

for the feminine privilege,
for the male right to the field.
Even that small task made me bleed.
Halfway between the flowered lap
of my grandmother and the black
heraldic silhouette of men
and machines on the golden field,
I stood crying, my ankle bones
raw and bleeding like the poppies
trussed in the corn stooks in their torn
red silks and soft mascara blacks.

(The recipe for my best bread,
half granary meal, half strong brown flour,
water, sugar, yeast and salt,
is copied out in the small black book)

In the black book of this parish
a hundred years ago
you will find the unsupported
woman had "pauper" against her name.
She shared it with old men.

The parish was rich with movement.
The woollen mills were spinning.

出于女性的特权，
因为男人适合下地干活儿。
甚至那轻活儿都让我滴血。
在祖母墓地长满花草
的山坳和洒满男人
及机器的黑色剪影的
金色麦田之间的半道上，
我站着哭泣，踝关节
擦伤流血，像罂粟花
被捆在玉米束堆上，由罂粟花那撕裂的
红丝绸和柔滑黑睫毛膏所点缀①。

（制作上好的面包，我的秘方是
一半全麦面粉、一半高筋棕色面粉、
水、糖、酵母和盐，
已抄写在黑皮小书内。）

这个教区的黑皮书内，
一百年前，
不难发现无助的
女性会有"贫民"字样在她名字旁，
她与年老的男人共享着它。

该教区过去处处生气勃勃。
毛纺厂机器曾旋转不停。

———————————

① 红丝绸指罂粟花的花瓣，柔滑黑睫毛膏指罂粟花的黑籽。——译者注

Water-wheels milled the sunlight
and the loom's knock was a heart
behind all activity.
The shuttles were quick as birds
in the warp of the oakwoods.
In the fields the knives were out
in a glint of husbandry.
In back bedrooms, barns and hedges,
in hollows of the hills,
the numerous young were born.

The people were at work:
dressmaker; wool carder; quilter;
midwife; farmer; apprentice;
house servant; scholar; labourer;
shepherd; stocking knitter; tailor;
carpenter; mariner; ploughman;
wool spinner; cobbler; cottager;
Independent Minister.

And the paupers: Enoch Elias
and Ann, his wife; David Jones,
Sarah and Esther their daughter;
Mary Evans and Ann Tanrallt;
Annie Cwm March and child;

水轮搅拌着日光，
织布机的敲打是所有活动
背后的核心。
梭子敏捷如鸟儿
穿梭在弯曲的橡林间。
麦地里把把金刀出鞘，
在农耕中闪耀。
在后排卧室、谷仓和篱笆内，
在那些山谷洞中，
诞生了数不清的年轻男女。

这些人曾在劳作，如：
裁缝、织工、缝被匠、
产婆、畜牧者、学徒、
佣人、学者、工人、
牧童、织袜工、裁缝、
木匠、海员、农夫、
毛纺匠、皮匠、佃农、
独立教士。

贫民如下：伊诺克·伊莱亚斯
和他的妻子安；大卫·琼斯，
他们的女儿莎拉和埃丝特；
玛丽·埃文斯、安·谭拉特；
安妮·凯姆·玛切和她的孩子；

Eleanor Thomas, widow, Cryg Glas;
Sara Jones, 84, and daughter;
Nicholas Rees, aged 80, and his wife;
Mariah Evans the Cwm, widow;
on the parish for want of work.
Housebound by infirmity, age,
widowhood, or motherhood.
Before the Welfare State who cared
for sparrows in a hard spring?

The stream's cleaner now; it idles
past derelict mill-wheels; the drains
do its work. Since the tanker sank
the unfolding rose of the sea
blooms on the beaches, wave on wave
black, track-marked, each tide
a procession of the dead.
Slack water's treacherous; each veined
wave is a stain in seal-milk;
the sea gapes, hopelessly
licking itself.

(Examine
your hands scrupulously

埃莉诺·托马斯，一名寡妇，住在凯葛格拉斯[1]；
莎拉·琼斯，八十四岁，和她的女儿；
尼古拉斯·利斯，八十岁，和他的妻子；
另一寡妇叫玛丽亚·埃文斯，来自圆形峪；
这个教区，工作稀缺。
因虚弱、年老、守寡
或母职，大家闭门不出。
在一个福利良好的国度，有谁
关爱过寒春中的麻雀？

如今河流更加清澈；它潺潺
流过被遗弃的磨坊轮；排水沟
排着水。自从油轮覆没，
海水泛涨，
漫过海岸，一波又一波
黑色，污迹，每一浪
均携带死者而来。
死水凶险；每一个纹理清晰的
波浪恰似海豹乳奶中的污点；
大海张嘴发怔，绝望地
舔着自己。

（仔细
检查你的双手

---

[1] 这是一所房子的名字。其威尔士语为 Cryg Glas，原意是粗蓝色。——
译者注

for signs of dirt in your own blood.
And wash them before meals.)

In that innocent smallholding
where the swallows live and field mice
winter and the sheep barge in
under the browbone, the windows
are blind, are doors for owls,
bolt-holes for dreams. The thoughts have flown.
The last death was a suicide.
The lowing cows discovered her,
the passing bell of their need
warned a winter morning that day
when no one came to milk them.
Later, they told me, a baby
was born in the room where she died,
as if by this means sanctified,
a death outcried by a birth.
Middle-aged, poor, isolated,
she could not recover
from mourning an old parent's death.
Influenza brought an hour
too black, too narrow to escape.

More mysterious to them

看看是否血中带污。
记得饭前洗手。）

在那座天真无邪的小农场里
住着雨燕和过冬
的田鼠，绵羊闯入
眉骨①，百叶
窗，是留给猫头鹰的门，
若射进梦想的螺栓孔。如今思想已逝。
末次死亡则是自杀。
一群低吟的奶牛发现了她，
他们渴求挤奶的颈铃如丧钟
敲响了那冬日的清晨，
当无人来挤奶时。
不久，他们告诉我，一个婴儿
出生在她死去的屋里，
仿佛如此神化，
便能一死唤一生。
中年，贫穷，孤立无援，
她无法从年迈母亲
之死的哀伤中复原。
流感持续了一个小时，
太黑、太窄而无法躲避。

更令他们觉得不可思议的

---

① 诗人将绵羊穿过的门比作眉骨，眉毛下的硬骨部分。——译者注

was the woman who had everything.
A village house with railings;
rooms of good furniture;
fine linen in the drawers;
a garden full of herbs and flowers;
a husband in work; grown sons.
She had a cloud on her mind,
they said, and her death shadowed them.
It couldn't be explained.
I watch for her face looking out,
small and white, from every window,
like a face in a jar. Gossip,
whispers, lowing sounds. Laughter.

The people have always talked.
The landscape collects conversations
as carefully as a bucket,
gives them back in concert
with a wood of birdsong.

(If you hear your name in that talk
don't listen. Eavesdroppers never
heard anything good of themselves.)

When least expected you catch
the eye of the enemy

是那个女人拥有一切。
一间农舍，栅栏围着；
屋内摆放着优质家具；
抽屉里藏着精美的床单；
花园里种满了药草和鲜花；
丈夫在劳作；儿子已长大。
她脑中乌云密布，心事重重，
他们说，她的死萦绕着他们。
实属匪夷所思。
我望向她的脸，
又小又白，从每扇窗户朝外看，
像坛中的一张脸。流言蜚语，
窃窃私语，声音低沉。掩口胡卢。

人们一直谈论着。
风景收集着各种对话，
小心翼翼如同提桶，
将他们归还时，与
一林子的鸟鸣声协奏。

（若你在聊天中听到自己的名字，
千万别听。偷听者绝不会
听到任何有利于自己的事情。）

最出其不意时，你捕捉到
敌人的眼光

looking coldly from the old world.
Here's a woman who ought to be
up to her wrists in marriage;
not content with the second hand
she is shaking the bracelets
from her hands. The sea circles
her ankles. Watch its knots loosen
from the delicate bones
of her feet, from the rope of foam
about a rock. The seal swims
in a collar of water
drawing the horizon in its wake.
And doubt breaks the perfect
white surface of the day.

About the tree in the middle
of the cornfield the loop of gold
is loose as water; as the love
we should bear one another.

When I rock the sea rocks. The moon
doesn't seem to be listening
invisible in a pale sky,
keeping a light hand on the rein.
Where is woman in this trinity?
The mare who draws the load?

冷冰冰地从旧世界里射出。
一个女人的命运应
取决于她在婚姻中的手腕；
对时间的秒针不再满足，
她便将手镯从双手上
摇取下来。海水漫过
她的脚踝。望着它圈成的结
从她细长的脚骨中
松开，从绕着岩石的泡沫绳圈上
脱落。海豹畅游
在环状水域中
拽着身后的地平线。
疑虑打破了白昼
那完美的白色表面。

玉米地正中央有棵树
周围，一个金圈
疏松如水；似爱那般，
我们应该宽容彼此。

我摇晃时，大海随之摇晃。月亮
仿佛并没有在倾听，
却隐藏在苍白的夜空中，
挥舞着一只轻盈的主宰之手。
在这三位一体中，女人身居何位？
拉货的母马呢？

The hand on the leather?
The cargo of wheat?
Watching sea-roads I feel
the tightening white currents,
am waterlogged, my time set
to the sea's town clock.
My cramps and drownings, energies,
desires draw the loaded net
of the tide over the stones.

A lap full of pebbles and then
light as a Coca Cola can.
I am freight. I am ship.
I cast ballast overboard.
The moon decides my Equinox.
At high tide I am leaving.

The women are leaving.
They are paying their taxes
and dues. Filling in their passports.
They are paying to Caesar
what is Caesar's, to God what is God's.
To woman what is Man's.

I hear the dead grandmothers,

皮革上的手呢？
小麦货物呢？
望着海路我感到
白色洋流愈加汹涌，
我浸没在水中，将自己的时间拨
至大海城钟的时刻。
我的抽筋、淹溺、能量
和欲望拽着满载的潮汐
网越过千礁万石。

膝部绕满一圈鹅卵石，不久
重量轻如一只可口可乐罐。
我是货物。我是轮船。
我将压舱物从船上抛下。
月亮决定我的昼夜平分点。
趁着高潮，我扬帆起航。

女人们将要离开。
她们正付清税费
和欠款，填报护照。
她们偿还凯撒、
上帝原属他们之物，
偿还女人原属男人之物。

我听到了已逝（外）祖母的声音，

Mamgu from Ceredigion,
Nain from the North, all calling
their daughters down from the fields,
calling me in from the road.
They haul at the taut silk cords;
set us fetching eggs, feeding hens,
mixing rage with the family bread,
lock us to the elbows in soap suds.
Their sculleries and kitchens fill
with steam, sweetnesses, goosefeathers.

On the graves of my grandfathers
the stones, in their lichens and mosses,
record each one's importance.
Diaconydd. Trysorydd.
Pillars of their society.
Three times at chapel on Sundays.
They are in league with the moon
but as silently stony
as the simple names of their women.

We are hawks trained to return

来自南威锡尔迪金郡的（外）祖母 [1]，

来自北威的（外）祖母，一个个皆在召唤

她们的女儿从麦地下来，

召唤我从马路进来。

她们拽着紧绷的丝绳两端；

派我们去取蛋、喂鸡，

将怨愤揉进自制的面包中，

将我们锁在沾满肥皂水的双臂中。

她们的碗碟洗涤处和厨房弥漫着

蒸汽、香味和鹅毛。

在我（外）祖父的坟头，

石头长满了地衣和苔藓，

记录着彼此的重要性。

助祭。司库。[2]

他们是当地的顶梁柱。

小教堂每周日三次礼拜。

他们与月亮结盟，

却如同他们女人的简单名字

那样安静，那样僵硬。

我们宛若一只只苍鹰训练有素，

---

① 南威尔士称（外）祖母为 Mamgu，称（外）祖父为 Tadcu；北威尔士称
（外）祖母为 Nain，称（外）祖父为 Taid。——译者注

② 助祭，威尔士语为 Diaconydd，英文为 deacon；司库，威尔士语为
Trysorydd，英文为 treasurer。——译者注

to the lure from the circle's
far circumference. Children sing
that note that only we can hear.
The baby breaks the waters,
disorders the blood's tune, sets
each filament of the senses
wild. Its cry tugs at flesh, floods
its mother's milky fields.
Nightly in white moonlight I wake
from sleep one whole slow minute
before the hungry child
wondering what woke me.

School's out. The clocks strike four.
Today this letter goes unsigned,
unfinished, unposted.
When it is finished
I will post it from a far country.

从圈子的外周返回
诱饵处。孩子们哼着
只有我们能听见的曲调。
婴儿划破水面，
打乱血液的旋律，让
所有感官丝丝
变得狂野。它的呐喊拽着肉体，淹没了
它母亲那乳白的田地。
每夜沐浴在皓白的月光里，我从梦中
缓缓醒来，足足一分钟，
在饥肠辘辘的孩子面前，
疑惑自己被何事惊醒。

学校已放学。时钟敲了四下。
今日此封信件并未署名，
尚未完成，还未投寄。
待完毕后，
我会从远乡将它寄出。

Daughter

A pearl, April, born of water,
borne now in the river's arms,
child of the mountain,
mermaid of the estuary,
everyone's daughter.
Let her not be lost to the mothering sea.
Let her be light on the wave.
Let her change us forever.
Let us see her sweet face whenever
we gaze on the river, the sea,
like the moon on water.
Let this pain that is sleepless
lighten to love, to kindness.
Let ours be the arms that caught her,
Love's weight, her light, the lightness
of everyone's daughter.

女儿

一粒珍珠，名叫艾珀，诞生于水，
如今殒殁于江河之中，
一座大山的孩子，
一条河口的美人鱼，
一位惹人喜爱的女儿。
愿她不会迷失在母爱般的汪洋之中。
愿她化作波涛上的柔光。
愿她永远地改变着我们。
每当我们凝视着江海，
但愿我们能看见她那秀美的脸庞，
宛若水中的一轮明月。
愿这无眠之痛
柔化为爱与善。
愿我们的哀伤化为双臂去拥抱她，
这份爱意、这道荣光、这份轻盈
理应属于那位人见人爱的女儿。

War and Death

战争与死亡

A Russian Woman in Tashkent, 1979

She stared at me with ice-blue eyes,
in my strange western summer clothes,
queuing to buy yoghurt in the street
in forty degrees centigrade.

Over her shoulder the glass city sang
with fountains, traffic, shifting sands,
the noon lament from a distant mosque,
a tremor at the city's root.

About us light was dazzling geometry,
shadows, bottomless wells of purple.
Air stood still as monuments
in sand, and heat, and snaking water.

Face to face under a dangerous sun
jostled by men of the desert, silk women
with their forty gleaming braids.
Her string bags slumped like beggars in the dust.

She took my arm, her Slav face serious.
In Tolstoy's tongue, she talked America,

1979 年塔什干市一位俄罗斯妇人

她用冰蓝的双眸凝视着我，
而我身穿奇异的夏日西服，
正顶着四十摄氏度的高温，
在街道上排队购买酸奶。

越过她的肩膀，这座玻璃之城扬起
歌喉，答和喷泉、车流、流沙之音，
附应远方一座清真寺飘来的晌午挽歌，
与城下根基的颤动共鸣。

围绕我们的光线似炫目的几何图案，
团团阴影，若口口深不见底的井。
在沙地、热浪和逶迤的水流中，
空气纹丝不动似丰碑。

烈日之下，迎面挤在人群之中，
一群生活在沙漠中的男人和梳着四十条
色泽光亮辫子并蒙着丝绸面纱的女人。
她的网兜耷拉着，像极了风尘仆仆的乞丐。

她拽着我的胳膊，一脸斯拉夫式严肃的表情，
用托尔斯泰的母语谈及美国、

and government, and war
"All we women want is peace."

And we embraced then, knowing nothing of the future,
only that our lands were far from there,
that about us moved on the pavements of the city
descendants of those tribes who took the silk road West.

That they had slept easy then in their encampments,
glimmering under starry desert skies, earth's skin
twitching harmlessly beneath them, before the foreigner
erected his monuments on a shifting earth.

政府和战争的话题：
"我们女人只想和平。"

而后我们相互拥抱，对未来茫然无知，
只知和平离我们的土地依然遥远，
只知身旁这些人行道上的行人，
其祖先是经由丝绸之路西行的部落。

只知他们曾在自己的营帐里酣然入梦，
在沙漠那片星光璀璨的夜空下熠熠烁烁，地表
在他们的身下挛缩，并无恶意；后来，这群外族
在这片不断流动的土地上树起了座座丰碑。

Six Bells

for the forty-four miners killed in the explosion on 28 June 1960

Perhaps a woman hanging out the wash
paused, hearing something, a sudden hush,

a pulse inside the earth like a blow to the heart,
holding in her arms the wet weight

of her wedding sheets, his shirts. Perhaps
heads lifted from the work of scrubbing steps,

hands stilled from wringing rainbows onto slate,
while below the town, deep in the pit

a rock-fall struck a spark from steel, and fired
the void, punched through the mine a fist

of blazing firedamp. As they died,
perhaps a silence, before sirens cried,

before the people gathered in the street,
before she'd finished hanging out her sheets.

六道钟声

缅怀 1960 年 6 月 28 日在板岩矿爆炸中罹难的 44 名
矿工

或许正在晾晒衣服的女人听见了什么动静，
她才停下手中的活儿，似突如其来的嘘声，

地球内部的脉动恰如心脏蒙受的一击，
而她仍旧怀抱着那水淋淋的

新婚床单和他的衬衫。或许
在刷洗台阶时一个个正抬头而望，

抑或将彩虹拧进板岩时一只只手戛然而止，
而当时在小镇的地下，在矿坑的深处，

一块坠石擦出了钢铁般的火花，引燃了
空腔，顺着矿井打出了一拳

灼热的瓦斯。他们罹难之时，
兴许死寂一片，不久警笛嘶鸣，

当地居民纷纷涌向街头，
而她正要晾晒新婚的床单。

Gleision

for the four miners killed at Gleision drift mine, 15 September 2011

Colours of mountain light, greens, greys,
blues of distance, dusk's lavenders.
Glâs of rivers and rain and waterways
where streams and heroes are lost
in the hill's dark hollowed heart,

and nothing's left but black of the bleak "if only",
the never again of men trapped in the pit
while women wait, and world grows lonely
at the slow procession of the hours, dread
of the imagined and remembered dead.

gleision: the plural of *glâs*, blue or green

青色的葛雷申煤矿

缅怀 2011 年 9 月 15 日在葛雷申露天煤矿罹难的四名
矿工

山光的颜色，或绿或灰，
或勾兑着远方的蓝和日暮的淡紫。
而川流、雨水和航道的青绿 ①
则使溪流和群雄淹没
在幽暗、空洞的山腹之中，

唯留下黯淡、凄凉的寄语"真希望……"：
愿不再有男性矿工被困在矿坑之中；
而世界在钟表那缓慢的嘀嗒声中
渐次寂寥，妇人个个望眼欲穿，生怕
想象中、记忆中的亲朋天人永隔。

---

① 诗人在英文原诗后提供了简短的注释：glâs 意为蓝色或绿色，gleision
是 glâs 的复数形式。此诗英文标题为 Gleision，既指颜色，又指煤矿名。因
此，汉译标题时按照音译和意译的原则忠实传达其意。葛雷申露天煤矿
位于英国南威尔士地区，具体在一个叫下塔尔波特港（Neath Port Talbot）
的郡级自治市内。该露天煤矿的四名威尔士矿工于 2011 年 9 月 15 日试图
用炸药将该煤矿的两个主体部分连成一体时，不幸落水溺亡。——译者注

Exhuming Your Father

Somewhere in a graveyard in broken Greece,
a man leans on his grief. A shovel, gloves,
a plastic bag. He doesn't own his plot
and the three-year rent is up. One he loves
lives here, in a few cubic metres of earth.
He brings the dead one, like another birth,

lifts the beloved, once father, once man,
reduced to a gather of earth and bone,
skull empty of all memory and mind,
the scattered fingers of a father's hand,
the all-is-forgiven warmth of their last hold
hardly faded from a son's reminding,

the loosening, letting go. His hands curl
on pins and needles, pearls.

挖掘令尊 ①

破败的希腊有座墓园，园内某处
一位男子依偎自哀。一把铁锹、一副手套、
一只塑料袋。他并不拥有自己的坟地，
而三年的租期已满。他深爱之人
长眠于此，在这几立方米的泥土中。
他带着逝者而来，仿若另一个新生，

他挖出心爱之人，曾经的父亲和大丈夫，
如今早已化作一堆泥骨，
颅骨清空了所有的记忆和思想，
手指骨也散落四处；
父子冰释前嫌而最后相拥的那份温馨
不曾从儿子的自我提醒、

松解、放手中消退。他的双手拳曲着，
麻痛难忍，如坐针毡，俨如珍珠。

---

① 此诗虽描绘死亡，却在忧伤的死亡主题中反映了父子之情，以及子对
父的深情留恋。——译者注

International Scope

国际视野

Tadzekistan

From the little plane
to Samarkand, rickety as a toy,
through gauzy heat a green geometry
glitters with miraculous white roses
of water on their silver conduits.

The image jumps
like old film under the rattling wing.
The desert, not gold as in children's books,
but mountainous and grey with stone-dust,
the cotton-fields laid out like carpets,

prayer rugs in the drought.
Walking, later, in the hot ash
of the ancient desert city, I see
the impossible silver battlements
of distant glaciers, and in the valley

water's quicksilver,
its Catherine wheels, its memory
of fern-designs that lean in wet places,
of feathers dropping from water-birds,

塔吉克斯坦

一架飞往撒马尔罕
的小型飞机，玩具般左右摇晃，
途经轻薄的热浪时，机上闪耀着一个
几何绿图，映衬着一根根银管上
那水珠绽开的朵朵奇妙的白色玫瑰。

在吱吱嘎嘎的机翼下方，
眼前景象跃动不绝恰如老式胶片。
这片沙漠，并非儿童读物所绘的金黄色，
而是千岩万壑，灰石叠尘，
此处棉田绵延不绝，犹似久旱之地中的地毯

和祈祷用的跪毯。
之后，行走在这座余烬般
焦热的沙漠古城中，我见到了
那些匪夷所思的银色城垛
宛若邈远冰川，在峡谷中，

发现了潺流的水银、
它的凯瑟琳之轮、它的追忆：
那些斜向潮润之地的蕨类设计、
从水鸟身上脱落的根根羽毛，以及

of dizzy vortices that know the way to spin.

It is melted mountain
come so far in the dark pipes and channels.
Yet it learns again the colour of the ice
it was. From here we look from the precipice,
hear a dog bark, a child cry, a cockerel crow,

see a Tadzek woman hang
clean cotton in the sun like any wife.
Let us praise hydro-engineers and five-year plans.
Let us praise the designer of ice-mountains glittering blue
on a far horizon like a wild idea.

一方方自我打转并令人目眩的旋涡。

它俨然一座被熔化的山峦，
从幽暗的管道和水渠中长途跋涉而来。
不过，它重新拾起了自己
曾经的冰色。从此处，悬崖边，我们俯瞰，
闻见犬吠、孩啼、鸡鸣之声，

望着一位塔吉克斯坦妇女在阳光下
如所有妻子一般晾晒洁净的棉絮。
多么卓越的水利工程师和宏伟的五年计划！
多么伟大的设计师，其奇思妙想
让冰山在远方的地平线上焕发璀璨的蓝光！

Neighbours

That spring was late. We watched the sky
and studied charts for shouldering isobars.
Birds were late to pair. Crows drank from the lamb's eye.

Over Finland small birds fell: song-thrushes
steering north, smudged signatures on light,
migrating warblers, nightingales.

Wing-beats failed over fjords, each lung a sip of gall.
Children were warned of their dangerous beauty.
Milk was spilt in Poland. Each quarrel

the blowback from some old story,
a mouthful of bitter air from the Ukraine
brought by the wind out of its box of sorrows.

This spring a lamb sips caesium on a Welsh hill.
A child, lifting her face to drink the rain,
takes into her blood the poisoned arrow.

Now we are all neighbourly, each little town
in Europe twinned to Chernobyl, each heart

邻居

昔春蜗行牛步。我们仰望天穹，
研习各种肩状等压线图。
鸟儿迟迟交配。乌鸦吸饮着羊眼。

成群小鸟从芬兰上空坠落，有在光中
留下朦胧签名的北飞歌鸫、
迁徙的鸣鸟，还有夜莺。

振翼终结在峡湾上空，每个肺似呷一口胆汁。
孩童皆被告诫：它们虽美却危险。
波兰被洒上了牛奶。每次争执

均是陈年往事的回爆，
一口苦味浓郁的空气，源自乌克兰，
由它那凄怆之盒放出的风吹来。

今春，一只羊羔在威尔士山岗上抿铙；
一位女孩儿抬起脸颊迎风饮雨，
仿佛将毒矢插入血液之中。

如今，我们互为睦邻，欧洲每座
小镇皆与切尔诺贝利毗邻，每颗心

with the burnt fireman, the child on the Moscow train.

In the democracy of the virus and the toxin
we wait. We watch for bird migrations,
one bird returning with green in its voice,

glasnost
golau glas,
a first break of blue.

golau glas: blue light

均牵挂着灼伤的消防员和乘坐莫斯科列车的孩童。

在一个病毒和毒气肆虐的民主国度，
我们翘首跂踵，望着候鸟迁徙，
希冀一只归来时携回绿色歌喉、

开放
蓝光 ①、
蓝之破晓。

───────────────
① 在英文原诗中，诗人用威尔士语 golau glas 来指代蓝光，并在诗歌末尾
给出英文对应词 blue light。——译者注

Ichthyosaur

at the exhibition of Dinosaurs from China

Jurassic travellers
trailing a wake of ammonites.
Vertebrae swirl in stone's currents,
the broken flotilla of a pilgrimage.
Bone-pods open their secret marrow.

Behind glass she dies, birth-giving.
Millions of years too late it can still move us,
the dolphin-flip of her spine
and the frozen baby turning its head
to the world at the last moment
as all our babies do, facing the storm
of drowning as it learned to live.

Small obstetric tragedy,
like the death of a lamb at a field-edge
the wrong way up or strangled at birth
by the mothering cord.
Perhaps earth heaved, slapped a burning hand

鱼龙

观中国恐龙展有感而作

这些侏罗纪的漂泊者
拖着一地鹦鹉螺般的化石。
其椎骨回旋在石流之中，
酷似一支残损的朝圣船队。
根根骨柱敞开隐蔽的骨髓。

玻璃背面的她已逝，却临盆在即。
数百万年来纵使姗姗来迟，它依旧扣人心弦：
她的脊柱如海豚般空翻，
而这个冰封的婴儿遭遇
溺水的风暴，在紧要关头，
如所有婴儿一般，将头探向
世界，因为它早已学会了生存。

分娩时的小悲剧，
恰似一只羔羊暴毙在田埂上，
也许因胎位不正所致，抑或
出生时被母亲的脐带所勒杀。
或许当他一头钻进她的门楣下躲避时，

on both of them as he ducked under her lintel,

leaving only a grace of bines

eloquent as a word in stone.

起伏的大地用一只炽热的手猛拍了下他们，
唯剩千娇百媚的藤萝
如碑文般传神动人。

Baltic

The air is white and dense
where fishermen dip their hooks
into black silence,
and it's hard to believe in islands
half a mile away in the mist,
the delicate archipelago of the map.

Six posts step out to sea, ice-locked
where water laps in summer,
and boats waltz on their slack ropes.
Salt-smells, fish, bird-cries
locked in the sea's cellar,
the land under wraps.

You can drive to Sweden, they tell me,
or catch the post for Stockholm half way over.
Trying to believe it, I walk on the sea,
out between the posts until I'm lost in whiteness,
wondering, without a bird's talent for magnetism,
how I'll know the way.

波罗的海

白色的天空弥漫着浓稠的气息，
渔夫们将他们的鱼钩
投入黑暗的静谧中，
难以置信
半英里以外的轻雾中，
便是地图上标注的纤细列岛。

六处邮筒眺望冰封的海面，
任凭夏日海水不停地拍击，
轮船舞动松垂的缆绳跳着华尔兹舞。
盐味、鱼腥味、鸟鸣声
均封锁在海洋的地窖中，
而这块陆地则被层层围裹。

我被告知：你可驱车前往瑞典，
或中途向寄往斯德哥尔摩的邮筒投递信件。
我信以为真，便行走在邮筒间
离岸的那片海域上，直到迷失在茫茫白雾之中，
心生疑惑：倘若无候鸟天生的磁场感应力，
我将如何识途，辨别航向？

Blue Sky Thinking

April 2010

Let's do this again, ground the planes for a while
and leave the runways to the racing hare,
the evening sky to Venus and a moon
so new it's hardly there.

Miss the deal, the meeting, the wedding in Brazil.
Leave the shadowless Atlantic to the whale,
its song the only sound sounding the deep
except the ocean swaying on its stem.

Let swarms of jets at quiet airports sleep.
The sky's not been this clean since I was born.
Nothing's overhead but pure blue silence
and skylarks spiralling into infinite space,

a pair of red kites flaunting in the air.
No mark, no plane-trail, jet-growl anywhere.

蓝天冥想

2010 年 4 月

我们重新来过吧：将飞机停航一段时日，
让出跑道给竞跑的野兔，
归还夜空给金星与明月，
崭新如初，仿佛不存在。

错失交易、不遑参会、缺席巴西的婚礼。
将清澈透明的大西洋还给鲸鱼，
它的歌声是探测深海仅存之音，
除了海水在它躯体上的摇晃声。

让成批的喷气式飞机在沉寂的机坪上沉睡不醒。
自诞生以来，我未曾见过如此洁净的苍穹。
头顶上方唯见一片澄明的蓝色宁静，
广阔无垠，听任云雀螺旋腾空翱翔，

任由红色纸鸢结对尽情飘扬。
处处无迹无痕，不见飞机行踪，不闻喷气轰鸣。

Lament for Haiti

For the ground that shivered its skin like an old horse,
for the shout of the sun,
the cry of the earth as it broke its heart,
the palace that fell into itself like snow.

For the hospital with its rows of white graves.
For the cathedral that folded on emptiness calling God's name
as it went.

For its psalms of sorrow,
the prayers of the living and dead.

For each crushed house, its cots, cushions and cups,
cooking pots pressed between pages of stone.
For the small lung of air that kept someone alive,
for the rescuer's hand, for the slip of a life from its grip.

For the smile of daylight
on a woman's face,
for her daughter dead in the dark.
For the baby born in the rubble.

海地挽歌

向老马般战战栗栗的地表致哀，
向怒吼的太阳致哀，
向呼号的大地致哀，因为它心碎肠断，
如同一座雪崩似的坍塌宫殿。

向医院里那一排排的白色遗体致哀。
向那座边呼唤上帝之名边往中空折叠的教堂
致哀。

向它奏响凄楚的诗篇致敬，
向那些为生者和死者祷告的人致敬。

向每座被蹂躏的屋舍及屋中被石板挤压
的婴儿床、坐垫、杯子和厨具致哀。
向使他人得以幸存的便携式水肺氧气瓶致敬，
向伸出援手的营救者致敬，向从手中滑落的生命致哀。

向强忍着阳光般
微笑的女人致敬，
向她黑暗中罹难的女儿致哀。
向废墟中诞生的婴儿致敬。

For tomorrow's whistling workmen
with their hods of bricks.
For scaffolding and walls rising out of the grave
over rosaries of bones.

向明日扛着砖斗、
吹着口哨的工人致敬。
向在一串串念珠般的遗骸上方
搭起坟茔的脚手架和围墙致敬。

Bodnant Garden

For Gillian Clarke

By Jingcheng (Peter) Xu

All flowers are smiling in glee,
whispering to the old yew-tree
the history of glory they've seen
writing spring, autumn, and winter
into this summer's flushed cheek.
The sky larks are to me greeting
like a magic of sweet welcome,
singing somewhere, near or far,
maybe in the aspens right there,
or in the thick bushes, always
unseen and yet never unheard,
with familiar children's echoing
from the lively Laburnum Arch,
breaking and cooling down the drowse
of heat: They have never been lost
or forgotten, nor have I since.
The beech tree overlooks the fall
down in the green valley that sprays

博德南特花园

致敬吉莲·克拉克

许景城

群芳争妍喜开颜，
朝着古老紫杉私语诉言
自己曾见证的荣耀历史，
将春光、秋韵、冬意一并
写入今夏那红润的脸颊之中。
一群云雀向我致意，
仿若一场甜美迎接的魔魅戏，
他们某处吟唱，忽远忽近，
或藏于那片白杨树中，
抑或浓密的灌木丛里，始终
身影难觅却鸣声不息，
稚童的回声似曾相识，
从喧嚣的金链花拱道传来，
击碎酷热所致的困意，送来阵阵
清凉：他们从未消失
或被遗忘，而我此后亦然。
那棵山毛榉树俯瞰着瀑布
顺着绿谷而下，将柔美乐曲

the soft tune to Lads-Love nearby.
Starlings hover the white Pin Mill,
doting on the red lotuses
that're sleeping sound in Lily Pond.

Even God would e'er love to dwell
in this amazing land that ends
with the unending love and peace:
The ending leads to no ending
but the beginning that well speaks—
The nature's mirror never breaks!

At Bangor University
June 8, 2017

洒向邻近的艾菊。
欧椋鸟翱翔于白色针坊上空，
觊觎着那朵朵酣睡
在百合池中的赤红睡莲。

甚至天神冀盼栖居
于此心旷神怡之地，尽享
无穷无尽的爱和祥和：
有涯之地通往无涯之境，
而万物复始正道言——
自然之镜未曾破残！

作于班戈大学
2017-06-08
译于白云山麓广外
2025-03-09

图书在版编目（CIP）数据

吉莲·克拉克诗歌精选译介：基于人类世生态诗学视角：英汉对照 / （英）吉莲·克拉克（Gillian Clarke）著；许景城译.—北京：知识产权出版社，2025.6.—（林苑"双龙"译丛 / 许景城总主编）.—ISBN 978-7-5130-9930-1

Ⅰ.I561.25

中国国家版本馆 CIP 数据核字第 20256PE927 号

责任编辑：杨 易	责任校对：谷 洋
封面设计：商 宓	责任印制：孙婷婷

吉莲·克拉克诗歌精选译介
——基于人类世生态诗学视角（英汉对照）

[英] 吉莲·克拉克（Gillian Clarke） 著 许景城 译

出版发行：**知识产权出版社**有限责任公司	网 址：http://www.ipph.cn
社 址：北京市海淀区气象路 50 号院	邮 编：100081
责编电话：010-82000860 转 8789	责编邮箱：35589131@qq.com
发行电话：010-82000860 转 8101/8102	发行传真：010-82000893/82005070/82000270
印 刷：北京九州迅驰传媒文化有限公司	经 销：新华书店、各大网上书店及相关专业书店
开 本：787mm×1092mm 1/32	印 张：13
版 次：2025 年 6 月第 1 版	印 次：2025 年 6 月第 1 次印刷
字 数：300 千字	定 价：79.00 元

ISBN 978-7-5130-9930-1